The BEDMAS Conspiracy

Deborah Sherman

Fitzhenry & Whiteside

Published in Canada by Fitzhenry & Whiteside, 195 Allstate
Parkway, Markham, Ontario L3R 4T8

Published in the United States by Fitzhenry & Whiteside, 311
Washington Street, Brighton, Massachusetts 02135

www.fitzhenry.ca   godwit@fitzhenry.ca

10 9 8 7 6 5 4 3 2 1

Library and Archives Canada Cataloguing in Publication
Sherman, Deborah (Deborah Faye)
The BEDMAS conspiracy / Deborah Sherman.
ISBN 978-1-55455-181-1
I. Title.
PS8637.H487B44 2011   jC813'.6   C2011-901397-5

Publisher Cataloging-in-Publication Data (U.S)
Sherman, Deborah.
The BEDMAS conspiracy / Sherman, Deborah.
[176] p. : cm.

ISBN: 978-1-55455-181-1 (pbk.)
1. Peer pressure -- Juvenile fiction.   2. Self-perception – Juvenile
fiction. I. Title.
[Fic] dc22   PZ7.S5476Be 2011

Fitzhenry & Whiteside acknowledges with thanks the Canada
Council for the Arts, and the Ontario Arts Council for their support
of our publishing program. We acknowledge the financial support
of the Government of Canada through the Book Publishing Industry
Development Program (BPIDP) for our publishing activities.

 Canada Council **Conseil des Arts**
for the Arts **du Canada**

 ONTARIO ARTS COUNCIL
CONSEIL DES ARTS DE L'ONTARIO

ANCIENT FOREST™
FRIENDLY

Preserving our environment
Fitzhenry & Whiteside Limited chose to print the pages of this
book on recycled paper and saved these resources':

	energy	water	greenhouse gases	solid waste
trees were saved for our forests	9 million BTUs	50,961 L	1,268 kg	371 kg

Printed by **Webcom Inc.** on
Legacy Hi-Bulk Natural 100% post-consumer waste.

'Estimates were made using the Environmental Defense Paper Calculator.

FSC
www.fsc.org

MIX
Paper from
responsible sources

FSC® C004071

Cover and interior design by Comm Tech Unlimited
Cover image by Tessa Dottor
Printed in Canada

The BEDMAS Conspiracy

Deborah Sherman

To everyone I begged, bugged, and bribed for opinions—a big thanks for all of your help.

—D.S.

Chapter 1

Mouldy Maple Syrup. Burrito Belches. The Broken Birthday Cakes. The possibilities were endless. The Rancid Chocolate Chip Cookies, Elegant Earwax, Repulsive Christmas Presents. It was easy once you got started. The Sloppy Saggy Scuzzy Sunbeams. Filthy Frothy Chocolate Sundaes. The Breathtaking Runny Noses.

"How about Nasty Kittens?" I offered.

"Not bad," answered Daniela.

"Vomit Comet?"

She frowned. "It rhymes—but it's gross."

"But aren't we *trying* to be a little gross?" I asked.

"A little," she agreed, "but that's a lot gross. The idea is to come up with a name that combines something nice and sweet with something icky."

Daniela and I had been brainstorming possible names for our band for the past hour. We hadn't yet struck the right balance between sweet and a little bit gross, but we were coming close. Trampled Ice Cream was my next offer.

"What about Melted Ice Cream?" countered Daniela. "Or we could really shock with the Barftastic Banana Splits!"

Our school, J.R. Wilcott Middle School, was holding its annual talent show next month. Wilcott's Got Talent had never been won by anyone from grade six. Usually a group of grade eights danced their way to the big prize. Occasionally, a grade sevener sang his or her way to the top. But I thought we had a good shot to take home the championship this year. My cousin Daniela was a great singer. I wasn't much of a musician but I was full of good ideas—really good ideas at this moment. I had it!

"Sick on a Snow Day!"

Daniela looked unimpressed. "Cute alliteration, Cuz, but it lacks the knockout, gross-out punch, don'tcha think?"

"Let me explain it to you, Daniela. If the idea is to combine something totally awesome with something rotten, what's better than being sick on a snow day? You wake up to find out that school's been cancelled due to a huge blanket of the white stuff, but when you try to yell for joy, nothing comes out of your dry, cracked mouth. Laryngitis! And when you try to jump out of your bed to start the good times, your legs are aching and your chest feels like it's on fire. The flu! It's a free day and you're *stuck in bed*. What's more of an awesome disappointment than that?"

"Sick on a Snow Day." Daniela slowly repeated the name.

It was important that I come up with a good name. I couldn't fake being musical, so I needed to make my mark with some solid ideas.

Daniela was still playing with the name. "Introducing, the one and only, Sick on a Snow Day," she sang out in a clear voice. "With two hit singles and a new CD about to drop, here's Sick on a Snow Day."

It must have worked, because she smiled. "Cuz, you are a genius! It's got the right mixture of elegance and trash. And you know how much I love alliteration! Sick on a Snow Day it is!"

Daniela had been living with my family and me for the past three months. Our moms were sisters, which made us first cousins. Daniela had spent the first part of the year with her parents in the South Pacific on an island called Papua New Guinea. Her parents were architects and they were building a hotel on the island. Daniela was supposed to go with them for the year, but after three days on that side of the world, she became incredibly homesick. After three months, her parents sent her home to live with us for the rest of the year. With long, red hair and a deep, strong voice, Daniela was lead singer material. Barely able to get through *Chopsticks* on the piano, I wasn't sure what material I was.

According to last term's report card, I could often be found gazing out the window, lost in a daydream, instead of paying attention to the teacher. Especially during math class. Every time Mr. Papernick started in on fractions, my mind automatically switched to a better place. And lately, this better place was onstage, winning Wilcott's Got Talent. Just thinking about math was enough to send me off. Multiplication tables and long division faded into the background until all I could see was Daniela standing on the middle of a large stage. She was swinging her microphone like a lasso. There I stood, front and centre beside Daniela, even though the piano is usually found off to the side of the stage. It was *my* fantasy after all. My fingers whipped up and down the keyboard as I crouched down to avoid being hit by the flying microphone. The floor shook as the audience jumped up and down. It was hard to hear Daniela over the cheering. She caught her microphone and put her arm around me. She was singing directly in my left ear.

"Earth to Adam," said Daniela, gently pushing my shoulder. "Wake up. Return to planet Earth, please."

I shook my head, trying to bring myself back to Daniela and our conversation. But she was lost in a dream herself.

"This could be my big chance," she said, looking right through me. "First, Wilcott's Got Talent, and then the lead in the Grade Eight Thespian Extravaganza Extraordinaire. Sky's the limit. Off-Broadway...Broadway..."

I had to cut her off. "Sorry to dash your dreams, Cuz, but you'll only be in grade seven next year. If my math is right, which it usually isn't, you'll have to wait another year to be the lead in the grade eight play."

"Not after they hear me sing!" said Daniela, smiling to herself and swaying to the music in her head.

Evidently, daydreaming ran in our family. I changed the subject to something more important. The band now had a name, a singer, and a piano/ideas man. We still needed one or two guitar players and a drummer. "My parents said we could use the garage for try-outs after school next week," I said.

"Why don't we have first auditions on Tuesday," suggested Daniela, "and then the second round on Wednesday?"

"I think we should have first auditions on Monday. Why wait?" I said. I was excited, and ready to get the show on the road.

"But we have a geometry test on Tuesday. I don't know about you," said Daniela, "but I need to study for it on Monday. Actually," she paused, "I *do* know about you because your dad has a very loud voice when he gets angry. You need to study for it, too—on Saturday, Sunday, *and* Monday!"

It was impossible to focus on numbers when the chance of winning a huge talent show loomed in my future. And in case winning Wilcott's Got Talent didn't provide enough distractions, there was the District Donnybrook Talent Competition, and—the ultimate— the City Championship. It was enough to send my mind spinning in a million different directions. But Daniela was right. My parents hadn't been impressed with my last report card. The whole street probably heard my dad when he saw all of the C's running up and down the report. I needed to force myself to open that math book and learn some numbers.

But I also needed to be sure that Sick on a Snow Day got first crack at Wilcott's top talent. I brokered a deal with my cousin. "I promise to spend the weekend learning formulas if you agree to hold auditions Monday and Tuesday."

I had worn her down. "Fine, but you better hold up your end," warned Daniela. "Your dad gets loud when he's mad. Now, excuse me while I wash my hair and work on my moves"—she tossed back her red hair with a dramatic shake of her head and used her tall, thin frame to strike a pose—"and you go learn a few new chords on the piano. I'm sick of hearing *Chopsticks*!"

We both had a lot of work to do.

Chapter 2

"The Swedish Meatball? What kind of act is that?" I asked Daniela.

"I think it might be a competitive eater," replied Daniela. "Gross, but highly watchable."

We were checking out the Wilcott's Got Talent sign-up list, which was posted on the cafeteria door. The deadline was Friday. It was only Monday, but the sign-up sheet was almost full.

"The Subtractions?"

"The math club's band."

"We Wuz Framed?"

"The guys in detention decided to form a break-dancing group. They've got a lot of spare time on their hands."

"WETPDA?" I asked, thoroughly confused.

"Wilcotters for the Ethical Treatment of Poor Defenseless Animals. You know, the guys who let the frogs out of their cages last year."

Those guys I liked! They got us out of our science dissections.

"I heard they were going to join forces with the guys from detention—they got to know each other pretty well—but I guess they decided against it," said Daniela.

Sick on a Snow Day only had two members, but the sign-up sheet was quickly becoming covered in ink. Two more acts scrawled their names on the list.

"The Flying Perogies?" I looked quizzically at my cousin.

"No idea!" laughed Daniela.

"I guess we'd better sign up before it's too late," I said to her. All this competition was making me nervous. I was seriously thinking about doubling my piano lessons. We signed up for the show even though our first auditions weren't until after school.

"Did you post all of the flyers?" I asked Daniela. We had made fifty flyers stating the date, time, and location of our auditions. I was hoping for a good turnout, especially after seeing the long list of competitors. On the bright side, it didn't look like J.R. Wilcott's marching band had entered. Perhaps we could find a drummer or tuba player who could keep the beat.

Daniela and I were just about head to homeroom when we heard a high, soft voice behind us. "We Wuz Framed—cool. Flying Perogies—nice! Sick on a Snow Day—what does that mean?"

It was Eldrick Hooperberg. He was a skinny little guy who really didn't fit in with anyone at school. Way too nerdy to be cool but not cut-throat enough to be a power-nerd, Eldrick just disappeared into the background. Supposedly, he was an alternate in the marching band, but there was almost no evidence of him in the school yearbook. A gigantic tuba player blocked him out of the photo. Things weren't much better in his class photo. His eyes were closed and his named was misspelled.

"Ellen Hopperbern?" wondered everyone. "Who's that?"

I didn't know Eldrick well. The only reason I knew him at all was due to Daniela. She had a soft spot for him. In the third grade, Eldrick had given her a bottle of liquid paper which he had dyed red to match her hair.

"He made the dye himself by mixing three different beetle juices," she said, flattered.

"That little new guy made it himself?" I had asked her at the time.

"Adam, we've gone to school with Eldrick since kindergarten."

I wasn't the only one who kept forgetting about him. Teachers were forever calling Eldrick up to the front of the class and asking him to introduce himself and tell us what school he'd transferred from. But Daniela had never forgotten his liquid-paper present.

"Poor guy," whispered Daniela, "I heard the Subtractions won't let him play the triangle in their rhythm section."

"Hey, Daniela. Hey, Adam," said Eldrick shyly when he spotted us. "I heard you guys are getting a band together. When are auditions?"

"First auditions are today. Second round is tomorrow," said Daniela.

"Why?" I asked. "Are you planning on trying out?"

Eldrick frowned and looked at the ground. He shuffled back and forth awkwardly. "Well, maybe not today. I'm tutoring Dez McDaniels in math and I've got to get him ready for the big math test tomorrow.

We've got a lot of work to do after school. But if it's okay with you, I'll come on Tuesday for the second round."

Quickly, I sized him up. Thick brown glasses, plaid button-down shirt tucked into a pair of brown cords that ended somewhere between his belly button and chest. He laughed nervously and pulled his pants a little higher. I wanted our band to be cool. Unfortunately, Eldrick was the opposite of cool.

Before I could try and talk him out of it, I heard Daniela saying, "Sure, no problem, Eldrick."

I nodded reluctantly. "See you on Tuesday, Eldrick."

A triangle player, no matter how good, was not what I had in mind for the band. I hoped today's try-out would yield some superstars.

Chapter 3

Sick on a Snow Day was officially in the talent show—which made it impossible for me to concentrate during class. I dreamed of bass guitars during biology. I fantasized about jamming throughout geography. Catchy choruses replaced chemistry formulas. By the time Daniela and I started walking home, I had written our first hit. I was just about to break into the chorus when, in the distance, I saw a bunch of people lined up on my driveway. This was good. Very good! We had the cream of J.R. Wilcott's crop to choose from.

As we approached my house, I saw Andrea Hackenpack tuning her guitar. Sal Gervano was twirling two drumsticks. Raz Keilberg strummed on his bass. Even some grade eights had showed up. Sludge Sludinsky was doing some serious stretching while Nat Kaplan hummed as she listened to her iPod.

We decided to hold auditions in alphabetical

order. Allan Alter was first up on drums. Daniela gently shook her head when he finished.

Andrea Hackenpack was next. She was one of the smartest kids at J.R Wilcott and great at everything she tried. But, she was also known to be a perfectionist and rather emotional. Daniela had once found her crying in the bathroom because she'd got an A-minus on her spelling test.

"I thought the teacher meant *presents* not *presence*," she had sobbed.

This was okay for me, because all great rock bands had one member who was a loose cannon. Andrea plugged her pink guitar into the amp and looked at us.

"Frieda and I are ready when you are."

"Frieda?" I asked.

"Frieda—my guitar. I believe a true musician should be *one* with her instrument. Frieda is my best friend. Jenny Mitchell was my best friend until I told her that I liked Michael Wise; and then she ran and told him, and then she ran back and told me that he said—"

"How about you and Frieda show us what

you two can do?" I interrupted. We had a long line queuing down the driveway that we needed to get through before dinner.

"My ex-best friend in Papua New Guinea did the exact same thing," said Daniela to Andrea. "Play for us now and you can tell me the rest later."

Andrea took a brief moment to compose herself. Then she looked down at Frieda and let out a howl.

"Okay, Frieda, let's do it!" yelled Andrea as her fingers started to work.

It was a beautiful friendship. Andrea's fingers plucked furiously and Frieda wailed happily in return. The faster Andrea's fingers moved, the happier Frieda sounded. Daniela bobbed her head up and down to the music. Andrea and Frieda were shoo-ins for Sick on a Snow Day.

Suddenly, we heard an off-key, tinny *twang*. It was followed up by a sharp *tongy twong* and then a limp *tangy tung*. Andrea stopped playing. Daniela and I looked at each other. Andrea glared furiously at Frieda. "I can't believe you're doing this to me right now!" she wailed. She stared accusingly at Frieda, who now sported two broken strings.

"Of all the times to let me down," hissed Andrea to her guitar. "True best friends are there for each other. You're no better than Jenny Mitchell!"

Andrea turned to us abruptly, "I'm sorry about this." She started to pack her bag.

"That's okay, Andrea," said Daniela, trying to soothe her. "Adam and I heard enough to know that you and Frieda are awesome." She looked at me and I nodded. "Can you have Frieda fixed by next week?"

"I don't think that's possible," said Andrea sadly.

"Well, what about the following week?" I asked. I was desperate to have her in the band. She was awesome and a bit loopy—the perfect band member!

"No, you don't understand," said Andrea. "After everything that happened with Jenny, I need a best friend I can *trust*. Frieda's proven herself to be just as untrustworthy as Jenny. I don't want to have anything to do with her again."

She handed us Frieda and started to button up her sweater.

"Maybe I'll take up the drums. The drums don't leave you hanging out to dry during your biggest moment. Yeah, the drums seem trustworthy. Solid and dependable. Or maybe I'll just buy a dog." She picked up her bag and headed out the door.

"Andrea, you forgot Frieda," Daniela called after her.

"Keep her," said Andrea without turning around.

Okay—so she was *a lot* loopy.

Daniela shrugged, "She was good, really good. But I think we just dodged a crazy bullet there, Cuz."

I had to agree, though somewhat regretfully. Andrea and Frieda really wailed.

Raz Keilberg, a new kid in grade seven, was next with his vintage bass guitar. It was a solid, if not spectacular, audition.

"Not bad," said Daniela.

"But we need more than 'not bad' if we are going to win this thing," I reminded Daniela. We already had one weak band member—me!

A slew of unimpressive guitarists were next.

"What do you think the chances are of Andrea forgiving Frieda?" asked Daniela.

We looked at poor Frieda lying broken and lonely in the corner.

"Don't count on it," I replied.

It turned out that Edward Nojna was a crack accordion player.

"Name any polka and I guarantee I can play it," he said proudly.

Farid Nazar was decent at keeping the beat on the recorder.

"He's worth keeping in mind," I said to Daniela, who looked doubtful.

"We might have to think outside the box," I told her.

Next up was Sludge Sludinsky. Sludge was a cool kid in the eighth grade. We were surprised to see him at our tryout. If there was a sticky situation at J.R. Wilcott, Sludge was usually in the middle of it. Toilet-papering the gym and placing stink bombs in the grade seven saxophones were two of his more memorable "extra-curricular activities." He could usually be found lounging in the back row of detention.

Recently, Sludge had wowed the whole school in the J.R. Wilcott production of *Romeo and Juliet*. Most people hadn't expected him to know who Shakespeare was, let alone want to perform one of his famous plays. But not only did Sludge learn the play (in detention, of course), he *really* surprised everyone by giving a terrific performance. In fact, he was so good that Principal Losman let him miss detention once a week so he could join the drama club. He was a bit of a Wilcott celebrity.

"Hey, it's awesome that you're here," I said, trying to sound cool. "What do you play?"

I don't think he heard me. He was staring at Daniela and his face was frozen in a goofy grin.

"Sludge, what instrument do you play?" I asked again.

He continued to gaze goofily at Daniela. I wasn't the only one who liked to daydream!

"Do something!" she whispered to me. Her face was as red as her hair.

I ran to the drum kit at the back of the garage and grabbed the cymbals. Their crashing noise jolted Sludge back to the real world. He turned his head to see where the clatter came from.

"Awesome looking skins, bro!" he said when he saw my brother's drum kit. "These are some sick tubs!" He took a seat. "What time do you want me to keep? Two-four? Six-eight?"

Daniela frowned helplessly at me. We had no idea what he was talking about.

I had to ad lib. "Your choice, Sludge. We just want to see what kind of skills you bring to the table... uh, *dude*," I added, trying to sound cool again.

Sludge twirled two drumsticks between his fingers. "One, two—one, two, three, four," he bellowed before starting to play. His left arm provided a speedy *boom* as his right arm offered a thundering *bop*. He played fast, furiously, and fantastically. I found myself clapping along as he attacked the drums. After a final whoosh of thumps and thuds, he tossed his sticks into the air, catching one behind his back and the other in his teeth.

Daniela and I were speechless. Sludge had to speak for us. "Will I get a call-back?"

There was no need for a call-back.

"You're in!" Daniela told him. "Welcome to Sick on a Snow Day."

Sludge grinned. "Awesome! So who's our axeman?"

Axeman?

"Who's playing guitar for us?" explained Sludge.

I really needed to bone up on my musical terms. "We're still looking," I told Sludge. "Andrea and Frieda broke up, so our axe person is undecided."

"Yeah, I saw Andrea heading into the dog pound. Do you mind if I sit in for the rest of the auditions?" he asked. "My dad has a garage band, so I know a little bit about this stuff."

Daniela and I happily said yes. Next up was Patrick Stoneman. He carefully took out his violin.

"Great squeak box!" enthused Sludge.

After Patrick came Amanda Tupper and her saxophone.

"Wild! She can really work that popsicle stick!" laughed Sludge appreciatively.

"Totally! One hundred percent!" Daniela and I agreed, pretending we knew what he was talking about.

It was almost dinner time. Auditions were winding down and we were still searching for two people who could play the guitar.

Sludge summed it up, "We gotta find some sidemen soon."

Last up were Beena and Meena Zellerpin. Identical twins, Meena and Beena were never far from each other. They had the same classes, ate at the same table, and had the same friends. They talked alike, walked alike, and ate alike—peanut butter and Swiss cheese sandwiches garnished with a dill pickle. They liked the same boys, hated the same food (pizza!) and finished each other's sentences. The only way to tell them apart was by their clothes. They dressed alike, of course, but Beena was always in blue and Meena was always in mauve.

"Blue. Starts with a B, just like Beena," explained Beena.

"Mauve. Starts with an M, just like Meena," said Meena.

Truthfully, most of J.R. Wilcott thought of them as one person—the Z's.

"Think they'll share a guitar?" whispered Daniela when they walked into the room.

Today they were dressed in polka-dotted skirts and fur-trimmed sweaters—Beena's, blue, and Meena's, mauve, of course.

"I hope you don't mind—" started Beena.

"—if we hold our auditions together," finished Meena.

Beena was holding a teal bass and Meena had a purple electric guitar.

"One, two—one, two, three, four," they counted off together before starting to strum. They played cleanly, quickly, and in perfect unison. Together, they swayed from side to side. They stopped playing at exactly the same moment.

"Do you guys mind if I beat the skins while you two do your thing?" Sludge asked the twins.

"Not at all," answered the Z's.

Beena's bass vibrated smoothly against Meena's slick guitar strokes as Sludge provided a steady beat. They sounded like they'd been practicing together for years, which in Beena's and Meena's case, was probably true.

Daniela and I looked at each other. It appeared we had our band: Daniela Olafson belting out the tunes; Sludge pounding the drums; Beena Z on her blue bass; Meena Z beside her on a mauve axe (I was picking up a lot from Sludge!); and, finally, Adam Margols playing one or two chords on the piano.

Sick on a Snow Day was set.

Chapter 4

My mom had made fried chicken for dinner. Usually, I'd devour three pieces before the rest of my family had even sat down at the table. But tonight I had bigger and better things on my mind.

"Shmick on a Shmow Shay ish shmoing to shwin thish eashily!" I was too excited to swallow my baked potato.

"Stop talking with your mouth full," lectured my mother. "We can't understand a word you're saying."

My older brother could. "You haven't even had your first practice yet, and already you're accepting the trophy," laughed Josh. "That's a lot of confidence for a guy who can only play two notes on the piano."

"Even I can play better than you, and I'm only seven," said my little sister Abigail.

"I might not be able to play well, but the resht of the shmand can," I replied, dribbling ketchup down my chin.

My cousin had better manners. She swallowed her food before joining in. "We've really got some good players. The Z's are amazing! You've got to hear them."

"The Z's," said my father. "Aren't they the identical twins who dress alike and talk alike?"

"You know, Uncle Stephen, I thought all they could do was pick out their coordinating purple and blue outfits, but it turns out they're amazing on their axes!"

"Axes?" asked my mom worriedly.

"We got Sludge playing the drums," explained Daniela.

"Yup, he pounds the skins for Sick on a Snow Day," I said as I tried to clean ketchup off the front of my shirt.

"Ah, that eighth-grade boy who likes Shakespeare and pulling fire alarms," said my mom, nodding her head.

"Well, I don't like the name, Sick on a Snow Day. It's stupid," said Abigail. I could always count on her to speak her mind whether I liked it or not.

"Now that you mention it," started Josh, "it does

lack a bit of pizzazz. Who came up with it?"

My mom knew how hard I'd worked at coming up with the perfect name. "I like it," she said. "Although I also like the name, *Studying for the Big Geometry Test*. No matter what you call your band, if you want to stay in it, there had better be an improvement in your marks, Adam."

My heart sank. I knew what my mom meant. I needed to prepare for tomorrow's big test. After dinner I tried, as my parents like to say, *to buckle down and study*. I really did! But it was impossible to concentrate on numbers when we had just assembled such a cool band. When it came to math, it was easier to think of music and just hope for the best tomorrow.

Chapter 5

I realized how much trouble I was in when I woke up the next morning.

"I'm so glad I learned the formulas Sunday night," said Daniela at the breakfast table. "I was too excited to concentrate on anything serious last night."

"Formulas?" I asked, in between bites of cereal.

"You didn't bother learning the formulas for today's test?" she asked incredulously. "How will you know how to find the surface area of a triangle or the volume of a sphere? How are you going to pass the test, Adam?"

She paused for a second. "Your dad is going to kill you!" she added, in case she hadn't made her point.

Panicking, I raced up to my room. I grabbed my math book, found chapter eleven and jotted down a few formulas on a small Post-It note. Hopefully I could learn them on the ride to school.

Unfortunately, Mr. Papernick was also my homeroom teacher. That meant I started every day off with mathematics. He was waiting for us with what looked to be a thick stack of papers. Nervously, I took my seat. I took out the little square of paper and scanned it quickly. I closed my eyes and tried to remember the formulas. Nothing. Again I looked at the paper and closed my eyes. *Nada*. Not one number.

Concentrating on school had always been a problem for me. But I had never considered cheating. Until now. The stakes were high. It was important I pass this test—more than important. If I wanted to be in the talent show, I needed to get a passing grade and keep my parents off my back. I promised myself it would only be a one-time thing. Just a few formulas that I would definitely learn at home tonight.

I stuck the Post-It up my sleeve. It was perfectly hidden. Mr. Papernick started to hand out the test. Allan Alter scanned the test and let out a depressed sigh. Jonathan Azam looked at the first page and put his head down on his desk. I was desperate! Just this once, I told myself again. I would make it up by doing extra equations for the next three weeks.

Mr. Papernick handed Andrea Hackenpack the test. Even straight-A student Andrea looked worried. I needed my cheat sheet!

I made a deal with myself. I would use the cheat sheet today, learn all of the formulas tonight, and then take the test again on the weekend. And do extra homework for the next three weeks. It seemed like a good deal. It would make up for the cheating, I told myself.

"Here you go, Mr. Laken," said Mr. Papernick as he handed his test to Sam Laken.

He was getting closer and closer to handing a test to Mr. Adam Margols. Me—a cheater. A cheater who was starting to sweat buckets. Beads of perspiration dripped down my neck. I wiped away the droplets. My hands were starting to tremble. Between the sweaty palms and the shaking, it became increasingly hard to grip my pencil.

Mr. Papernick headed down my row. "Good luck, Ms. Mackie," he said as he gave Darcy Mackie the test.

In a few seconds, I would have my test and I would cheat my way to a passing grade. My pencil slipped from my sweaty grip and rolled on the floor. I reached down to pick it up. But my sweaty, shaking fingers made it hard to grasp. After what felt like an eternity, I finally managed to pick it up. But, by the time I did, I realized I couldn't go through with my plan. I may have been a daydreamer who couldn't add, but I wasn't a cheater. I would just have to fail the test and deal with my parents.

I bolted from my seat and headed to the garbage can. The illicit sticky note was giving me a big, psychic paper cut. I just wanted to get rid of it. I was ready to take the test and get a good old-fashioned F. My parents would be angry but I'd promise to do extra math every night—perhaps even get a tutor. Maybe I could take a re-test next week.

My hands were still wet with perspiration. Just three steps away from the garbage pail...

"Hey," said a squeaky voice. It was Eldrick Hooperberg. "You dropped something, Adam."

Eldrick leaned over and picked up the little yellow piece of paper which had somehow unglued itself from inside my sleeve and slipped to the floor. He waved it above his head, formulas flashing for all to see. Panicking, I looked Eldrick directly in the eye, hoping he'd realize he should clam up. He completely ignored my signal.

Mr. Papernick wasted no time swooping in. "Well, well—what have we here? I'll take that, Mr. Hoopenbaum."

"Hooperberg," corrected Eldrick weakly.

"It appears we have ourselves a cheat sheet, Mr. Margols." Mr. Papernick frowned as he studied it. "Though I'm not sure if this sorry attempt would have improved your chances of getting through this test."

"But...I...*aargh*." I tried to protest, but my voice seemed to have stopped working. I was in big trouble. At best, I would have to set up camp in detention. At worst, I would be grounded forever. And how could I be in a band if I could never leave my room? There was a good chance that my dream of winning Wilcott's Got Talent was over.

Why, oh why, couldn't Eldrick Hooperberg have kept his mouth shut? A brainiac like Eldrick would have known exactly what that piece of paper was. He'd brought me down—on purpose—and I was never going to forgive him! My eyes shot daggers at him as Mr. Papernick sent me away to the office.

Chapter 6

My day quickly went from bad to worse. First, I had to sit through a lecture by Principal Losman. Then I had to write the test in the office and wait for Mr. Papernick. When he came at recess, he gave me his own lecture. Two lectures were not ideal, but I could have lived with it if it was my full punishment. It was not. Mr. Papernick concluded his speech with the seven words no kid ever wants to hear: *I'll be speaking to your parents tonight*. He didn't look very happy.

For the rest of the day, I wavered back and forth on cancelling band practice. Sweat trickled down my forehead every time I imagined Mr. Papernick's phone call—and my parents' reaction! In the end, I decided to hold practice. Most likely I'd be saying goodbye to a lot of privileges for a very long time. There was no sense starting my grounding early. Although it was hard, I tried to put my desperate situation out of my head and concentrate on the band.

"Your parents are going to be furious when they hear about this," said Daniela as we walked home.

"I feel like barfing just thinking about it," I confided.

"So do I—on your behalf," said my cousin.

Luckily, the rest of the band quickly showed up for practice and cut short our queasiness.

"I really don't like the name Sick on a Snow Day," said Beena as she plugged in her teal bass.

"Me neither," said Meena as she tuned her mauve guitar.

"Since we brought it up," said Sludge, "I'm not wild about it either. It lacks a certain *coolness* factor. What does it mean, anyway?"

I tried to dazzle Beena, Meena, and Sludge with the idea behind our name.

"Something gross combined with something cool," repeated Sludge when I finished my explanation. He looked like he was thinking it over. "Have you considered Nasty Kittens?"

The twins still weren't convinced either, but I didn't want to waste valuable time discussing our name. "Let's call it a 'working name' for now.

If someone comes up with something better, we'll definitely consider it," I suggested.

The twins agreed. It was time to concentrate on the music. Daniela handed out some sheet music she had downloaded off the internet. We took on the first song—a popular one on the radio—and sounded pretty good!

"I think it's important that we have some original music," I told everyone after practice as we sat in the garage, drinking Cokes and munching on snacks.

"Totally, bro," agreed Sludge. "Ed Nojna told me the Flying Perogies are writing an original rock opera.

That sounded hard to top.

"We Wuz Framed have choreographed an interpretive dance where they fight against Principal Losman's punishment for not doing your homework," said Beena.

"Totally true," confirmed Meena. "They literally break-dance their way out of detention."

"Well, rumour has it that the Subtractions are going the other route. They wrote a song called 'Losman Is Tops, Man,'" said Daniela.

"What a bunch of suck-ups," laughed Sludge.

Suddenly, there was a timid knock on the garage door. I got up to answer it. There, holding a gleaming triangle, stood my new mortal enemy, Eldrick Hooperberg. I tried to shut the door but he jammed it open with his triangle wand.

"You said I could try out today," he reminded me meekly.

"Forget it," I told him. I was trying to keep my cool and not blow a gasket in front of the band.

"But a triangle will add charm to your music," tried Eldrick.

"Then *I'll* play the triangle and the piano," I said firmly, attempting to hold my temper in check.

"But I don't just play the triangle. I'm an auxiliary percussionist," he said.

"I don't know what an auxiliary percussionist is and I don't care," I responded flatly.

"I play the tambourine, finger cymbals and ratchet—you know, anything you can hit or scrape. Except the drums," he added hastily as Sludge opened his mouth to protest. "I work *with* the drummer." His list was met with silence. "I can write lyrics, too," he offered as he stared at the tops of his shoes.

"So write some lyrics and then hand them in to Mr. Papernick," I said acidly.

He looked helplessly at Daniela. "But—"

"But nothing!" I yelled at him, finally blowing my stack. "Do you know how much trouble I'm in because of you? Mr. Papernick is probably speaking to my parents right now! As long as I am in this band—and that might not be for long—*you* are not. Find another band to bother."

Eldrick was staring at his shoelaces like they were telling a very sad story. "I thought you might need an all-city percussion champion," he mumbled.

"We don't, so you can go," I replied curtly.

He left without another word. I turned to Daniela. She wasn't smiling. "You were pretty hard on him, don't you think?"

"Daniela, I'm going to have to spend weeks in detention because of him! Weeks that could have been spent practicing the piano, you know. You think he can do no wrong because he made you a dumb bottle of coloured liquid paper in grade three. Wake up and see the big picture here."

"Don't use that tone with me, cousin," said Daniela angrily.

We might not have been brother and sister, but we could fight like we were. We argued back and forth until Sludge finally banged on his drum.

"Time out!" he called, getting our attention. "Remember us? Care to explain what's going on here? Who was that little guy and what did he do to make you so mad?"

"He's the new transfer from Greer Street Middle School," said Beena to Sludge.

"No," corrected Meena, "from Everett Elementary."

In all of my anger, I had forgotten about Sludge and the Z's. They were huddled together, wide-eyed with surprise at the sudden turn of events. Not being in my math class, they were clueless about my eventful day. Reluctantly, I told them the whole sorry story.

"I was *throwing away* my cheat sheet," I stressed, "and he just up and waved it around in front of the class. I'll never forgive him—not that I'll ever have the chance when my dad finds out. He'll probably kill me.

"That's rough," sympathized Sludge.

"*Really* rough," agreed Beena and Meena.

It was hard to concentrate after all of the drama. We agreed to call it a day and have another practice Sunday morning—barring my punishment, of course. We also agreed to start working on some lyrics. The goal was to be practicing an original song by early next week. Daniela and I watched the rest of Sick on a Snow Day hop on their bikes and cycle home. When they were dots in the distance, I turned to Daniela.

"How could you do that?" I asked accusingly. "Aside from making me look bad in front of the guys, how could you think I'd want that *rat* in the band?"

"I'm sorry, Adam. I just felt bad for him. He really wants to be part of a group, especially after being dissed by the Subtractions."

Suddenly, my mom popped her head in the door. My heart plummetted into my stomach. That earlier feeling of nausea was back. I gripped Daniela's arm tightly.

"Dinner in one hour," she called cheerfully. It was a strange tone of voice to use with your soon-to-be-in-big-trouble son. I waited for her to continue: no television, no PlayStation. But that was all she said.

"The calm before the storm?" wondered Daniela.

Our fight was quickly forgotten. We united as we prepared for the upcoming battle. My parents didn't say anything about the subject when we sat down to eat. I tried to read between the lines.

"Adam, can you pass the potatoes, please?" asked my dad. Was he trying to catch me off guard before coming down with the hammer?

"Do you want more chicken?" asked my mom. Was she trying to fatten me up before sending me to my bedroom for the next month and a half? Maybe I'd got lucky and Abigail or Josh had accidentally deleted the message. Perhaps I was off the hook? It sure seemed that way.

I managed to relax a bit and eat dessert.

But my luck gave out after dinner. My parents waited until I was strategically trapped between them on the couch.

"Your dad and I love you, Adam," began my mom.

Uh oh! With an opening like that, I knew I was in for some trouble.

"But we were shocked when we spoke to Mr. Papernick," finished my dad sadly. It was never a good sign when they did the old double-teaming tactic.

I tried to interject, "But I was *throwing away* the cheat sheet. I wasn't going to cheat!"

"Yes, Mr. Papernick told us that side of the story, too, even though he isn't totally convinced that you weren't going to cheat. However, we know you and we love you—so we are willing to give you the benefit of the doubt there, Adam. We'd like to think that you know right from wrong. But we're disappointed you went so far as to *make* a cheat sheet," said my mom.

My cheeks flushed. Knowing that they trusted me at least that much meant a lot.

"The truth is, your school work has been terrible all term," said my father, finally getting to the crux of the matter. "The fact that you felt the need to make this cheat sheet is proof that you knew you were unprepared to write the test. We did a little investigating and found out you took an 'incomplete' on your last book report and history assignment."

I couldn't believe they'd talked to all my teachers! The walls were suddenly closing in. Now my bedroom looked like it might become a jail cell. For a moment there, I had been hoping for a mild, two-week sentence with time off for good behaviour; but now the situation was looking grim.

"We're worried about this, Adam. Do you remember last term's report card?" My mom had it in her hand just in case I didn't. She read aloud. "Mr. Papernick called you a daydreamer. Mr. Kagan said you had a vivid imagination but didn't use it in your English assignments. Ms. Pemberley said you were clever in history but didn't apply yourself. She wondered what you were always gazing at out the window. And now, you're so focused on this new band. We're worried you're forgetting that you have other commitments—first and foremost, school. We're thrilled you found something that interests you so much. But—"

This 'but' was not heading to a good place. I tried one last time, "I didn't—"

"Adam," said my mother seriously. I knew

better than to argue with Mom when she used that tone of voice. "We support your dreams, dear, but it's our responsibility to make sure you don't neglect your school work. So…"

Here it came.

"…we've set some targets that we're sure you can reach—*motivational* targets."

Motivational targets! This did not sound good.

"B's on all of your tests and assignments."

"Including math?" I asked, panicking.

"Including math," answered my parents together. My mom continued. "We've arranged to have regular meetings with Mr. Papernick to make sure you're staying focused."

"But, Mom, Dad, what if I can't reach these targets?" Even though I knew the answer, I had to ask.

"Then you'll have to leave the band," said my father sympathetically. He seemed to be taking this harder than my mom.

I could barely breathe. Getting B's in all of my classes would take hours of studying! I felt like I was choking in a room full of smoke.

"Take a big breath," said my dad.

I tried gulping back some air. This deal meant tons of work, especially if I wanted to fit in weekly piano lessons. It wouldn't have mattered if they had taken away my TV and PlayStation privileges, because I had no more free time! But I didn't have a choice. If it took a report card of B's to win Wilcott's Got Talent, then a report card of B's it would be.

I turned to my parents and gave them a weak smile. "Well, I guess I gotta start on my homework if I'm going to reach my motivational targets." But inside, I wasn't smiling. Worried, I headed to my room to try and make sense of that mess of numbers called algebra.

Chapter 7

Luck seemed to be on my side. I got a B on my geography test and eked out a B-minus on a spelling quiz. My parents weren't happy about the B-minus.

"You didn't tell me what *kind* of B I had to get," I argued successfully. "Think of it as a B with decorations."

But even better than my grades was the fact that Sludge had turned out to be a genius at song-writing. He'd written "Detention Blues" overnight and we had been practicing it ever since.

"I'm not sure about this," Daniela confided to me at first. "Did you notice the lyrics?"

She sang them to me:

> *I'm just a girl with flaming red hair*
> *Singing to you that things aren't fair.*
> *Falling for a guy from the wrong side*
> *of the 'hood*
> *Between us, many weeks of detention*
> *stood.*

After school I was free as a bird
But he was trapped until December 3rd.

The Detention Blues, oh so blue
And you're also grounded, too.

Pulling the fire alarm wasn't so bad.
The principal shouldn't have been so mad.
Maybe he can cut your sentence short
If you write an eight-page book report.

The Detention Blues, oh so blue
And you're also grounded, too.

Maybe you'll get out at the end of May
And then we can go to a nice café.

"He wrote a love song about me!" Daniela concluded, sounding a little alarmed.

"You don't *know* it's about you. Sure, you have red hair, but there are a couple of strawberry-blondes in our school," I pointed out. "And, yes, maybe Sludge served a lengthy stint in detention last year for pulling a false fire alarm, but I heard he had a few accomplices. Maybe the song is about one of them? One of them and Nat Caplan? She is sort of red-haired-ish if you look closely at her highlights."

Daniela was still reluctant. "I don't know if I can go in front of the school and sing a love song about me and Sludge."

But, after practicing the song a few times with the whole band behind her, Daniela had to admit the song was special. The melody was perfect for her low voice and the chorus was stick-in-your-head catchy. Sludge had written a kicking solo for Meena and a simple piano part I could cope with easily enough. Even my siblings thought we sounded good.

"Keep practicing—you'll be fine," said Josh.

"Not awful!" agreed Abigail.

Sludge had done some stealth scouting. "I heard the Flying Perogies jamming and they sound pretty tight. And we need to watch out for Marty Jenkins, the Swedish Meatball. Competitive eating is always a hit with the audience."

We decided to up our practices to four times a week.

"Are you sure you'll be able to keep on top of your schoolwork?" asked Daniela doubtfully.

"Let *me* worry about that," I told her. "*You* just worry about hitting those high notes at the end of the song."

The competition was right around the corner. I was doing my best to clear my mind of guitars and amps and focus on numbers and letters. But it was a struggle.

Chapter 8

On the morning of the competition, something about Daniela just didn't seem right. First, I heard retching noises in the bathroom, followed by a long flush of the toilet. She looked pale as she went into her bedroom and closed the door behind her.

"You can do it. You'll be fine," I thought I heard someone say to her. But when I opened the door, Daniela was alone.

The plan was for the band to wear coordinated outfits. The Z's agreed to drop the mauve and the blue so we would all be dressed alike in black pants and funky tuxedo t-shirts.

"Daniela, your t-shirt is on backwards," said my mother as we came down for breakfast. She started to pour six glasses of juice.

"No breakfast for me, Aunt Elisha. I'm not hungry. I'll just meet you guys in the car," said Daniela as she went to fix her t-shirt. Her legs seemed wobbly as she left the room.

She didn't say more than two words during the

drive to J.R. Wilcott. When we arrived, we went straight to the gym. The bands in the talent show were allowed to perform a sound check. The Z's were already there, bubbling with enthusiasm.

"I thought blue was my best colour," said Beena, "but I love these black-and-white shirts."

"Me, too!" enthused Meena.

Sludge was busy setting up his drum kit onstage. He waved when he saw us.

"What's up?" he said when I reached him.

"I'm worried about Daniela," I confessed. "She's not acting like herself. She hasn't eaten anything and she's barely said a word to me."

Sludge looked over at Daniela, who was slumped against the wall.

"Look at her—she looks like she might pass out!" I said, panicking.

"Don't worry," said Sludge, trying to calm me down. "She'll be fine once she sings the first few bars of 'Detention Blues.' You know," he confided, "she doesn't know it, but I wrote the song for her."

$$(\, ^2 \, / \, x \, + \, - \,)$$

We were the last band to have a sound check, but when

it was our turn, Daniela was nowhere to be found.

"I think I know where she is," said Beena heading to the girls' washroom. She emerged with her arm around our shaky lead singer.

"I'm okay," Daniela muttered. "I'll be fine."

She wobbled over to the microphone. Sludge counted the beat and we launched into "Detention Blues." Sludge had a point: the song was written for Daniela and it was perfect for her. Even though Daniela wasn't at her best, she managed to pull it off. But as soon as we were finished, she collapsed into a chair backstage.

A few minutes later, the doors opened and kids flooded the gym. Soon, the room was packed with students and teachers. Our school president, Michael Wise, took the stage and explained the rules of the competition.

"Remember, Wilcotters, *you* choose the winner. Cheer as loudly as possible for your favourite act," he told us, "so we can crown them champs and send them on to the District Donnybrook." The room roared with approval. Michael smiled. "Let's get the show rolling with Wilcotters for the Ethical

Treatment of Poor Defenseless Animals singing their original song, 'Frogs are People, Too.'"

WETPDA hopped onstage in matching green outfits. The competition was on! After they croaked out a few notes, we realized that WETPDA was better off sticking to protests. Their performance was met with weak applause. We Wuz Framed, four guys from the back row of detention, fared a bit better with their interpretive break-dance. While the guys weren't naturals, Wilcotters appreciated anyone who challenged Principal Losman's strict policy on homework. The audience cheered as We Wuz Framed moonwalked their way out of detention.

Wilcott's Got Talent was frontloaded with musical acts. The Subtractions were next with their tribute to our principal, "Losman is Tops, Man." Principal Losman grooved to the beat, but the song didn't go over well with the rest of J.R. Wilcott. Light applause was mixed with a smattering of boos. Averagely Mediocre performed decently, but was a bit lacklustre.

Genevieve Simon was next. She had recently been the female lead in Wilcott's Great Eight

Extravaganza Extraordinaire. She had played Juliet to Sludge's Romeo.

"Not a bad smoocher," Sludge had told me privately.

The play had been a smashing success and Genevieve was sticking with what worked. Her arms waved wildly as she recited a passage from the play. She flung her head from side to side dramatically. She laughed; she cried; she threw herself on the ground all in the name of Shakespeare. But, as a solo performer, Genevieve didn't have what it took to move the audience. Only her friends clapped.

The next few acts weren't very memorable: three dance crews, a juggler who only juggled two balls and a tap dancer from grade eight.

Next up was grade sevener Brad "Mumbles" Fedkowsky. His nickname said it all. Teachers were always asking Brad to speak up because they couldn't understand him.

"My tlunts spkn bkwrds," muttered Mumbles.

"Can't hear you!"

"Speak up, Brad!" yelled a few people from the audience.

"His talent is speaking backwards," yelled his

59

best friend, Marc Rosenberg, from the back of the gym.

Mumbles began to warble. "*Dunal evitan duna emoh ruo adanac o.*"

As usual, we couldn't understand a word coming out of Mumbles's mouth. A bunch of kids turned to Marc. "What's he saying?"

"He's singing 'O Canada' backwards," said Marc proudly. "You go, guy!" he yelled encouragingly to Mumbles.

Up next was our real competition, the Flying Perogies. They ripped into their rock opera, "Filled with Potato and Cheese." Sludge was right. They were awesome. Ed Nojna had cracked their line-up and, believe it or not, was wowing the school with his mad accordion skills. As he launched into a rocking solo, the rest of the band laid down their instruments and started to hop up and down. They waved their arms and encouraged the room to get up. Wilcotters quickly got up on their feet and joined the party.

Ed was finishing with a burst of accordion staccatos when Daniela turned to me and quietly said, "I can't do it."

"Excuse me?" I said, pretending I didn't hear her.

"I can't go up and sing in front of the whole school. I just can't, Adam."

"What do you mean, you can't? You *have* to," I told her firmly.

The Flying Perogies packed up their instruments. Competitive eater Marty Jenkins prepared to take the stage.

"I thought I could do it," said Daniela with tears in her eyes, "but I can't."

I looked into Daniela's eyes and realized she was in real trouble. "But what about the moves you've been practicing at home for hours and hours in front of the mirror?" I asked, doing one of her little shimmies. "Who'll get to see them?"

"I can't go up in front of everyone and have them all staring at me. I just can't." She started to sob helplessly.

I didn't know what to do. Marty was explaining the finer points of competitive eating to the audience. He opened a giant vat filled with meatballs.

"One hundred and one Swedish meatballs," he told the audience. "And I am going to eat them all in the next seven minutes. The audience gasped in a combination of anticipation and disgust.

Daniela wiped her nose on the sleeve of her tuxedo shirt. "I'm so sorry, Cuz. I wish I was someone else, but I'm just a coward."

Suddenly I had an idea!

"You *can* be someone else!" I told Daniela confidently. "Come with me."

With everybody in the gym, we made a quick trip to the drama room without being noticed. In the prop basket, I found a short, blond wig which I quickly slapped over Daniela's red ponytail. We looked in the mirror.

Maybe.

Then I added a pair of dark, oversized sunglasses.

Perhaps.

I tied a red scarf around her neck.

We were getting there.

Finally, I added a leather jacket.

Now we were in business!

Beside me no longer stood Daniela Olafson. Staring back at us in the mirror was the *new* lead singer of Sick on a Snow Day!

Chapter 9

The wig completely transformed Daniela. Sick on a Snow Day's old lead singer was a tall girl with dramatic, long, red hair. Our new lead singer was a lanky Scandinavian boy with a blond bowl cut and cheesy taste in sunglasses.

"You're a new person," I told her as I tucked the rest of her ponytail up under the wig's elastic meshing. "Olaf Danielson—our distant Swedish cousin. No one will ever know it's you. You're free to go up on stage and rock."

She was staring in the mirror. "You think?" she asked.

"I know!" I replied confidently. It was our best shot.

"I'm not sure," she said, playing with her posture, trying to hunch her shoulders and appear less feminine.

"No time to worry. We're up next," I said pushing her out of the room. I could hear cheering coming from the gym.

We passed a couple of girls at the water fountain.

"Hey, Adam," said a grade seven girl whose name I couldn't remember. "Who's your friend?"

The girls were smiling at Daniela. I nudged Daniela in the ribs and she smiled at me with growing confidence. "You can do it!" I assured her.

The closer we got to the gym the louder the yelling got. "Ninety, ninety-one, ninety-two!"

The crowd was in a frenzy. Marty was nine meatballs away from reaching his goal. His cheeks puffed out with meat. He looked like a chipmunk.

"Ninety-three, ninety-four!"

"Ugh, I think I'm going to be sick," said Daniela.

"Take a deep breath," I told her. "The stage fright will pass in a sec."

"It's not the stage fright," she said. "It's Marty and those meatballs. I can't watch!" She covered her eyes.

Daniela and I did our best to get backstage. We needed to find the rest of the band and let them in on the plan. But it was difficult. Wilcott was going berserk.

"Ninety-eight, ninety-nine!"

Marty was on meatball 100 when we finally got backstage. He picked up meatball 101 and gazed at it. I noticed he was looking a bit green. He hesitated. For a moment, I thought I might have enough time to gather the band and give them the scoop. But then he popped the meatball in his mouth, swallowed, and raised his arms in the air. The room went wild.

"Stay hungry!" yelled Marty as he exited the stage with his fists still in the air.

It was our turn!

"We've been looking all over for you!" huffed Sludge. "Where's Daniela?"

"Look, this is—"

"Hey, he's cute," said Beena.

"Really cute," agreed Meena. Beena and Meena smiled at "Olaf."

Sludge knew something wasn't right. "Wait a sec—" he began.

"Yeah," I interrupted. "*This* is Daniela. But today she's our cousin, Olaf. From Sweden. I'll explain later."

Sludge looked our new lead singer up and down. "Cool!" he decided.

We took our places. As Sludge knocked his drumsticks, I started to wonder if Daniela would be able to pull off our Swedish switcheroo. I wasn't worried about her singing. Her voice was low and husky. And, while I was proud of my quick thinking, I began to doubt if a simple wig and a pair of sunglasses could cure Daniela's stage fright.

I stole a look at Daniela. I tried to catch her eye but she was staring at the ground. Instead of starting the song, she let the introduction run long. I started having a mini freak-out. What if Daniela's vocal chords were paralyzed with fear? Shooting a few sideways glances at each other, Beena, Meena and Sludge did their best to go with the flow. We repeated the introduction to "Detention Blues."

Was Daniela going to faint? I debated running over to catch her fall. Slowly, she raised her head. Finally, she looked out into the crowd and glared fiercely. Raising her arms dramatically, she wordlessly demanded that all of J.R. Wilcott get on their feet and clap. My new cousin Olaf was working the room! With the crowd clapping rhythmically, Daniela started to sing the first line of "Detention Blues."

Suddenly my stomach sank. The song! Sludge had written "Detention Blues" for *Daniela*. It would make no sense if it was sung by a guy. Luckily, Daniela proved to be very quick on her feet. She changed the lyrics on the fly:

> *I'm just a dude with blond hair*
> *Singing a tale about things that*
> *aren't fair*

She continued to improvise.

> *A girl falling for guy from the wrong*
> *side of the hood*
> *Between them many weeks of detention*
> *stood.*
> *After school she was free as a bird*
> *But he was trapped until December 3rd.*
>
> *The Detention Blues, oh so blue*
> *And he's also grounded, too.*

Wilcotters loved it! They clapped to the beat as Daniela strutted around the stage. They swooned as she crooned and shimmied and shook. She even pulled a grade sixer up on the stage to dance with her. Feeding off the energy, Meena ripped into her guitar solo. She electrified the room. Finally, Daniela dropped to her knees and looked into the crowd. Together, they sang the final chorus:

> *The Detention Blues, oh so blue*
> *And he's also grounded, too.*

Sludge came out from behind the drums. Sick on a Snow Day joined hands and took a bow. The crowd roared with appreciation. "Olaf" took an extra bow and the room went wild! Finally, we left the stage. In the end, the contest wasn't even close. Backstage, the other acts were gracious about our victory. Marty lay on the ground, wastebasket nearby, but he gave us the victory sign.

"Great lyrics," said Rocks Mudman of We Wuz Framed. "Everyone knows what it's like to be stuck in detention."

"When did that blond kid transfer here?" asked Kristian Bloch of WETPDA. "We could use someone with his charisma to help us head up our new campaign, 'Totally Tofu/No Pigs in Pigskin.'"

I was saved by my lead guitarist and bassist. Meena grabbed one of my arms and Beena grabbed the other. Together, they propelled me into a corner where

Sludge was already waiting. I had some explaining to do. I gave them the quick version of events.

"I never would have picked Daniela to have stage fright," said Meena. "If anyone, I thought it would be you freaking out about your piano playing."

"Me, too," echoed Beena. "Quick thinking with the costume change, Adam. She looked great. I didn't really believe it was Daniela until she started to dance at the end."

Sludge was a bit disappointed. "I wrote the song for *Daniela*. And now it's being sung by some Swedish dude named Olaf. I mean, I know it's Daniela—but it's just weird, man."

Where was Daniela anyhow? Another pair of hands grabbed my arm. Expecting my cousin, I spun around and grabbed…Principal Losman.

"Congratulations to you, too, Adam," he laughed. "Well-deserved, although I had hoped The Subtractions' song might have fared a bit better."

I smiled at him, not really listening. Where was Daniela? I craned my neck trying to search for her.

"I'd like you and Daniela to meet me in my office in fifteen minutes so we can talk about that new lead singer of yours," said Principal Losman. "I heard his name is *Olaf*?"

My neck quickly snapped back into place. I tried to appear casual as Principal Losman looked at me.

"See you in fifteen," he reminded me.

I quickly went off to find my cousin—the red-headed one.

Chapter 10

"**M**aybe we should tell him the truth?" suggested Daniela.

"No way," I replied. I had found Daniela and we were taking the long way to Principal Losman's office. "If we tell him the truth, we might have to give our crown to the Perogies," I reasoned. "I've got a better idea. We make up some story about Olaf doing an exchange program for the semester."

Daniela frowned, "What am I supposed to do for the next few months? I can't go around and pretend to be Cousin Olaf. The wig was really itchy and my Swedish accent stinks."

"Don't worry," I reassured her. "I'm pretty good at thinking on my feet. I came up with Cousin Olaf in the first place, didn't I? And on such short notice, too," I added pointedly, as we approached Principal Losman's office.

We knocked and opened the door a crack. Principal Losman was sitting at his desk filling out some papers. I wasn't sure, but I thought he was humming the chorus of "Losman is Tops, Man." He waved us into the two chairs in front of his desk.

"I wanted to talk to the two of you about your new lead singer," he began.

"You mean, Cousin Olaf," I said trying to appear in control of the situation. "He's our cousin from Scandinavia. Sweden, actually. You know—the country north of Denmark, south of Norway. Part of the Great Kingdom," I floundered. I was beginning to regret turning down Sludge's offer to pull the fire alarm and buy us some time to come up with a plan. But I figured we were in enough trouble already.

"Daniela," said Principal Losman, "I thought *you* were the lead singer of Sick on A Snow Day. What happened?"

I could tell Daniela wanted to come clean about her stage fright. Principal Losman was actually decent—for a principal—and he was looking at Daniela with understanding eyes. Before she could open her mouth, I interrupted.

"Cousin Olaf is actually our cousin on our mothers' sides. Their brother, Sam, once went over to Sweden on business. Computer stuff, I think. He fell in love with a stewardess and married her right when they got off the plane." The story didn't sound too bad so far. I looked to Daniela for support. She nodded at me to go on. So I continued, "Our parents decided cousin Olaf should come here on exchange. So he can learn all sorts of new stuff."

Principal Losman smiled. "Indeed."

"Our school is a really good place...to learn new stuff," I said lamely.

"Really good," added Daniela, realizing that I was struggling.

"Especially if you have Mr. Papernick for math," I added. "That man really knows his numbers."

"But Olaf is not enrolled at J.R. Wilcott," said Principal Losman. "How can he be on an exchange program if he's not coming to our school?"

Evidently, Principal Losman was going to be a tough nut to crack.

"It's a *special* exchange, Principal Losman. He's here to learn about North American culture. Instead of going to school, he does things like…"

"…go to the mall," ad-libbed Daniela.

"Yeah! Totally!" I agreed enthusiastically. "He goes to the mall and then writes a report comparing our stores to Swedish stores. Then he emails the report to his school in Sweden."

"It's a very *advanced* exchange program," added Daniela.

"He also sees movies here and then compares them with the ones back in Sweden. Same with hockey games and donuts."

The story sounded solid. In fact, *I* wanted to go on this cool new exchange program. I was sure Principal Losman was buying it hook, line, and sinker.

"So how did Cousin Olaf get involved in the band?" he asked, his mouth twitching at the corners.

"My throat started to feel sore last week," fibbed Daniela, coughing a bit for good measure. "It got worse and worse until I didn't think I'd be able to sing. Adam and I knew that Olaf has a good voice."

"We hear him in the bathroom every morning," I quipped.

"It was a last-minute solution," said Daniela, "but we were desperate."

"As you heard earlier, Principal Losman, the guy can sing." I added.

"Fantastically," said Daniela. "He's got a great low register and wow, can he hit those high notes!"

"So we invited him to join the band," I said, cutting Daniela off before she gave herself away. "I'm sorry we didn't tell you. It was a very last-minute thing."

Principal Losman's lips twitched some more. "That sounds like some exchange program. Comparative donut analysis? I think I might sign myself up next semester."

Then he started laughing. The jig was obviously up.

"You knew the whole time?" I asked.

"I knew the whole time," he confirmed. "But I never knew you had such a good imagination, Adam. Comparing donuts!" He started chuckling again. "I think you should give creative writing a shot, young man."

Daniela and I nervously waited for him to continue. On the one hand, he was laughing; on the other, he *had* called us into his office. We waited for the fallout of our attempted deception.

"I've got one last question for the two of you. If there were no sore-throat issues, why did you do it?"

Daniela took a deep breath. "I don't know what happened to me, Principal Losman. I woke up this morning paralyzed with stage fright." She seemed relieved to finally tell the truth. "As much as I wanted to go onstage, as much as I had prepared, I just couldn't do it." Then she told him how my idea cured her jitters.

"Impressive," commented Principal Losman.

Daniela pleaded one last time, "The chance to sing in front of the school means so much to me, Principal Losman. Please don't make me let down the band. We worked so hard for this."

"Olaf will appear at the District Donnybrook and that will be it," I told him. "Then he'll be on a plane to Sweden. We promise."

Principal Losman thought for a minute and then smiled. "I can see how much you love performing, Daniela, in spite of the stage fright. And how important it is not to disappoint your friends. Your secret is safe with me. I won't reveal your cover."

Daniela and I smiled at each other in relief.

He continued, "But you need to keep this situation in check. Olaf will be responsible for his own education. Let's call it 'self-directed learning.' In other words, he won't be attending any classes at J.R. Wilcott, understood?"

We nodded. The Swedish sensation was back in town!

Chapter 11

After school, we found Sludge and the Z's in the back of the cafeteria, celebrating with ice-cream sundaes. They were toasting each other with vanilla, chocolate, and hot fudge.

"Daniela," asked Beena, "what *happened* to you?"

"Yeah, what *happened*?" echoed Meena.

Before we could explain, we were surrounded by half of our grade six classmates. The female half!

The first to approach us was Janine Stroop. All of grade six knew she was boy crazy.

Janine got right to the point. "Olaf is totally hot. He *is* Sick on a Snow Day."

"Is it true that he's come all the way from Norway?" asked Lisa Hutchin, popping up behind her.

"Sweden," corrected Daniela.

"And he's involved in an exchange program where he hangs out at the mall?" questioned Janine and Lisa's best friend, Sarah Hibbit.

"Yup," I answered quickly, trying to shoo them away. "He's there right now."

Janine looked at Sarah and Lisa.

"He's going to need help finding the stores with the best clothes," said Lisa.

"And the coolest music," said Sarah.

"Don't forget about food," said Janine.

"To the mall!" agreed all three girls as they walked away.

I had managed to tell the rest of the band about Daniela's case of stage fright right after our meeting with Principal Losman. Of course, I'd also filled them in on my quick thinking. Sludge and the Z's were so impressed that they'd wasted no time in spreading the legendary story of Cousin Olaf around the school. They weren't as impressed, however, when I set up our practice schedule.

"Four practices a week?" said Sludge. "I'm not exactly one for school, but I'm going to need a little more time to get my homework done, dude. I'm finished with detention this week and I'm hoping to enjoy a little sunshine before I get sent back there."

Beena and Meena agreed with Sludge. Daniela

wanted to support me, but even she agreed our practice schedule was a bit intense.

"The District Donnybrook is in a few weeks," I reminded them. "The competition will be stiffer than the Subtractions and Averagely Mediocre." Seeing my point, the rest of the band nodded. "Right now, we need to focus on the competition and worry about school stuff later. Trust me, lots more homework and tests will be waiting for us after the competition."

I must have been convincing because the band eventually agreed to all of the practices—even the one on Monday, the day before the big spelling test. Beena and Meena left the cafeteria and headed to the library to study. Daniela went to talk to Mr. Papernick about something she didn't understand in the previous day's homework. Sludge dug deep into the bottom of his bag and fished out a beat-up history text book. I looked at him with a raised eyebrow.

"Just trying to manage my time better, bro," he smiled.

Soon, I was left sitting alone. I noticed blabbermouth Eldrick Hooperberg heading my way. He looked like he was walking with a purpose. His expression was determined—or at least as determined as he could muster. There was no way I was going to let him ruin my perfect day. I gave him a dirty look. Before he could open his mouth, I grabbed my stuff and darted out of the cafeteria.

Chapter 12

That evening, my family surprised me and Daniela with a celebratory chocolate cake.

"To the band," toasted my mom as we all clinked glasses of apple juice.

"To Olaf!" toasted Abigail.

"Did I ever tell you about *my* high school band?" asked my dad, doing the moonwalk. "We lasted three weeks before breaking up. The usual band politics: our sound, our lyrics, whether to sing in French or English."

Josh bolted after wolfing down three pieces of cake. Daniela had already excused herself to wash her hair. My mom "suggested" that Abigail go watch TV. Something was up.

She got right to the point. "We still have a deal, Adam. District Donnybrook or not, we are holding you to it."

"I've done everything you said," I told them. "I've gotten some sort of B on all of my tests."

"We spoke to Mr. Papernick and he told us that you're not paying attention in class again. He says you're scribbling in a notebook instead of listening to him," said my dad.

"No more writing lyrics in class," ordered my mother.

"But I've learned tons of new words from writing so many new songs," I argued. "Last week, I was working on a protest song about the crummy food in the J.R. Wilcott cafeteria. It was really hard to find words that rhyme with lasagna, banana and hoagie, but I managed to do it and learned that Banya is a little village in south-east Bulgaria, Ghana is a country in Africa, and Muskogee is a town in eastern Oklahoma, on the Arkansas River. I'm totally going to ace the next geography test!"

"Yogi also rhymes with hoagie," said my dad. "A guy who practices yoga. You could have used that. Or maybe, instead of asking for hoagies you could have just used a more common name like submarine sandwich and then shortened it to 'sub.' A lot of words rhyme with sub—tub, cub, rub, club. Hey, you could have worked in *club sandwich*." He started to hum a few notes.

My mom elbowed him sharply in the ribs.

"Right," he said getting back on track. "It's great that you're getting familiar with the globe, Adam, but we have an agreement. B's in all of your classes. Regardless of whether you're in a superstar band or not."

"You have a spelling test next week," said my mother.

How do parents know everything?

"If you don't get a B on it, your practices will be cut."

"But the Donnybrook is in a few weeks! We need to practice every day!"

"You'll just have to find a way to make time for both school and the band," said my mother firmly.

There was no arguing with them. This amazing day had suddenly gone south—and it was about to get worse. I had barely made it out of the room before the phone rang. It took me a couple of seconds to recognize Lisa Hutchin's voice. It sounded much more nasal on the telephone. I held the phone away from my ear.

"He wasn't there!" she whined.

"Who wasn't there, Lisa?" I asked, confused. Lisa and I weren't close friends. In fact, she had never called me before.

"Olaf!" she wailed.

I held the phone even further away from my ear.

"Huh?" I was still confused. "Where was he supposed to be exactly?"

"The mall. Sarah heard from Janine who heard from Raz Keilberg that this week, Olaf has to write a report comparing North American french fries to Swedish french fries. I went to every french-fry stand in Orchard Mall and couldn't find him." She lowered her voice a bit. "Can you keep a secret?" She didn't wait for my answer. "I think Olaf likes me. I could feel a real *connection* between us when he sang."

I didn't know what to tell her. "Well, Lisa, I *think* he said he was going to Orchard Mall, but to tell you the truth, his mouth was full of cereal when he told me what he was doing today. Combine that with his heavy Swedish accent, and maybe I misunderstood. He could have said Everton Mall or even Aldershot Mall. I really don't know."

I tried to change the subject. "Want to hear some

of the new lyrics I've been working on?"

"No, thanks," she answered quickly before hanging up.

Ten seconds later the phone rang again. This time it was Sarah Hibbit. I repeated the story about being unable to understand Olaf when he talks with food in his mouth. Sarah was also uninterested in hearing my new lyrics. So were Janine Stroop, Jenny Mitchell, and Marlene Tang. Exhausted and sick of talking about the mall, I finally told my parents to tell any grade six girl who called that I wasn't home.

But I hadn't mentioned the grade six boys. I had one more disastrous phone call coming my way that night.

"Adam, telephone!" called my mom from the kitchen.

I was sitting in my bedroom, trying to find a word that rhymed with casserole.

"I'm not taking any more calls!" I yelled back at her.

In some houses, people actually stood in the same room when they wanted to talk. But not in my house. We just yelled through the walls.

"You said you didn't want any more phone calls from *girls*," she bellowed from the bottom of the stairs. "It's not a girl this time."

She was getting closer to my bedroom, but we were still a floor apart. I picked up the telephone.

"Hello," I said wearily.

"Um…uh… hi, Adam," said the person on the other end of the line. I didn't recognize the voice immediately. It sounded a bit confused and unsure, which was weird because whoever it was knew he was calling me. Why should he sound so confused?

"I, uh, need to talk to you about something."

I started to notice a high-pitched quality to the voice. I still couldn't place it, but I knew I had heard it before.

"It won't take too long," said the voice.

Then I noticed a *tattletale* quality to the voice. Eldrick Hooperberg!

"Do you have a minute?" the voice almost pleaded.

It was the mouldy cherry on my now miserable sundae of a day.

"You'll want to hear what I have to say," he said as firmly as possible for him.

"There's nothing you can say that I am interested in," I told him wearily.

"You'll talk to me if you don't want me to say anything about Swedish Cousin Olaf—or should I say, Cousin *Daniela*," said Eldrick.

So he knew the truth about Daniela. Great! I was too exhausted to deal with Eldrick right then, but I figured it would be a good idea to find out if he had a plan hidden up his scrawny sleeve. After all, snitching was part of his repertoire.

"Fine, meet me at my locker tomorrow morning," I said, hanging up before he had a chance to respond.

I went straight to Daniela's room and knocked on the door. But it wasn't Daniela who answered. It was Olaf!

"What do you think, Adam?" asked my new Swedish cousin.

Daniela was wearing the blond wig and she had a new black fedora perched on top of it. She wore a pair of funky red sunglasses and black vinyl boots. Lisa, Sarah, and the rest of the girls at school were going to go crazy!

"I went to Orchard Mall after school and picked up a few things," said Daniela. "But it was hard to get a moment to myself. I swear every girl in the sixth grade was at the mall today. And they kept bugging me to tell them where Olaf went. Finally, I gave in and joined Sarah in the hunt for him."

"He's become pretty popular," I agreed.

"Want to see what else I bought for our famous, Swedish, rock-star cousin?" she asked.

I nodded enthusiastically, forgetting all about my morning meeting with Eldrick Hooperberg.

Chapter 13

Eldrick was waiting for me at my locker.

"You've got twenty seconds," I said to him flatly.

"I know the truth about Daniela," he said quietly.

"And what exactly is that?" I said, playing along with him.

"That she's Cousin Olaf."

"So?" I waited to see where he was going with this.

He was getting ready to play his hand. "I'll stay quiet about it if you give me something in return."

"Yeah? And what is it that you want?" I waited for some stupid request like a date with Daniela or to stop giving him dirty looks when he passed by my locker.

"I want to join Sick on a Snow Day."

Finally, he had shown his cards—and he was carrying the ace of blackmail! His plan was so bold that I was almost impressed.

He mustered up all of his courage. "Let me play

triangle in your band or I'll tell the whole school the truth about Olaf."

"And what if you did?" I said, calling his bluff. "You think the rest of the school really cares if it's Daniela or Olaf who's singing?"

"Yes! And I suspect that it's not just the rest of the school that will care if Olaf ceases to exist. What about Daniela? I'm guessing that she needs him," said Eldrick. "Besides, look around, Adam."

I looked to the right and saw Lisa, Sarah, Janine, and about a dozen other grade sixers. They had the Z's cornered.

"Where will he be today?" demanded Sarah.

"Is he going to be at Aldershot Mall?" asked Lisa and Sarah.

I looked left.

"I bet he can dunk a basketball. Remember when he jumped off the amp? The guy can fly," I heard Joe Jacobs say as he hobbled by on crutches. Joe was captain of the Wilcott basketball team. He had torn up some cartilage in his left knee last week.

"And did you see his scissor kicks?" said Joe's best friend, Anil Kapul. "I bet we can recruit him for the track-and-field team. We could use him in the 100-metre hurdles."

I looked back at Eldrick. "Okay, so he's popular. But it still doesn't mean that I'll let you in the band."

"Look at the bulletin board," commanded Eldrick.

It was wall-papered with blue and yellow flyers—the official colours of Sweden. Looking closer, I read the thick, black text: *Vote Olaf Danielson for President.*

I was confused. "We already have a school president."

"I heard some kids talking. They think he'd make a good president because 'Detention Blues' really captures how they feel about school."

"He didn't even write the song!" I said.

But it didn't matter. I looked around and took in the whole scene. Joe and Anil were drawing up basketball plays for Olaf. Janine cornered Meena and demanded to be told Olaf's whereabouts. A bunch of grade sevens walked by wearing the same type of oversized sunglasses Olaf wore onstage. Eldrick was right. Olaf was the most popular guy in school!

"Your band is good," said Eldrick. "But your Swedish singer makes it great. We voted for you because of Olaf. All the girls love him and the guys think he's super cool. Who will support you at the District Donnybrook if there's no Olaf? No one from Wilcott will show up and cheer for you and you know it. In fact, everyone will be really mad if they find out you duped them. You'll have no chance of winning the District Donnybrook if you don't have the school behind you."

Eldrick had me trapped.

I tried a new tactic. "You would blow Daniela's cover? You would really do that to her?"

"I really want to be in this band," he answered simply.

I still wasn't positive if he would rat us out, but I had no way of knowing for sure. I played my last card. "We've already written all of our material and there are no triangle solos."

"Don't care," said Eldrick, smiling. "I'm an *auxiliary percussionist*. I can play a bunch of instruments."

Out of the corner of my eye, I could see

something yellow and blue flying from the school flagpole—the Swedish national flag.

I sighed. Eldrick was in.

Chapter 14

As I headed to band practice, I debated what to tell Daniela, Sludge, and the Z's. I didn't want to admit I had been blackmailed.

Triangles—they're the new electric guitars. Too much!

Triangles—I wanted to funk up the band for the Donnybrook. Not believable enough.

An auxiliary percussionist will add layers to our sound. Maybe. It was just technical enough to sound believable.

As it turned out, I didn't need any excuses. Eldrick was already there, holding court with the rest of Sick on a Snow Day. They must have assumed that the two of us had solved our differences.

"Great idea—" started Beena.

"—to add an auxiliary percussionist," finished Meena.

Eldrick smiled shyly.

"The more instruments, the merrier," agreed Sludge.

They were still riding high from our victory.

"Nice," whispered Daniela in my ear. "I'm glad you two have made up. I knew he wouldn't have turned you in on purpose."

I gritted my teeth and nodded.

"I've been thinking about our name," said Eldrick, gaining confidence. "It kind of lacks *pizzazz*, doesn't it?"

Sludge and the Z's nodded vigorously. Daniela shot Eldrick a look. For once, he was smart enough to shut up.

"Listen," I told the band. "I only have an hour, so we'd better make it count."

"Hot date?" grinned Sludge.

"With a dictionary. I need to ace the next spelling test, but I just can't get my head around these stupid I's and E's. Who really cares? *Ugh*. And I'll be eighty by the time I figure out the way to spell *because*."

The Z's nodded in sympathy.

"If only I could remember the word list as easily as I remember our lyrics!" I joked.

Eldrick reached into his pocket and retrieved this week's word list. "*Neighbour, weigh, friend, receive, dessert, because…"*

"Why am I not surprised?" I mumbled to no one in particular.

"Meena, Beena, when I got in here you guys were messing around with a few chords on your guitars. Can you play them again?"

The Z's grabbed their instruments and began to play. It sounded pretty good. Eldrick glanced down at his word list and cleared his throat. Daniela glanced at me. What was he up to?

He started to sing.

Geography, Algebra, English and History—
Why we get so much homework is a mystery.
It takes up all of our precious free time.
Is having an hour for PlayStation such a crime?

Big Elephants Can Always Understand Small Elephants. Yeah Yeah Yeah.
Big Elephants Can Always Understand Small Elephants. Yeah Yeah Yeah.

There are so many things I could do in
those hours after dinner:
TV, computer games, web design for a
beginner,
Calling the cute girl in homeroom or
playing sports—
Instead I'm stuck inside writing book
reports.

Big Elephants Can Always Understand
Small Elephants. Yeah Yeah Yeah.
Big Elephants Can Always Understand
Small Elephants. Yeah Yeah Yeah.

He sang the chorus one more time. "I call it 'The Homework Tragedy.' It's kind of a companion piece to 'Detention Blues'."

I had to admit the tune was kind of catchy, but the lyrics made no sense. "Big elephants can always understand small elephants? What does that even mean? It doesn't go with the rest of the song."

"*B*ig *E*lephants *C*an *A*lways *U*nderstand *S*mall *E*lephants," repeated Eldrick, slowly and deliberately. "Put the first letters together and you get BECAUSE. It's a little study trick I use. You said you wished you could remember this week's word list as easily as you remember our lyrics. You should have no problem if the lyrics and the word list are one and the same."

The idea wasn't half bad.

"Play it again, E!" bellowed Sludge.

The band started up. After they sang the chorus, Sludge chimed in:

I before E, except after C—I just need some time to be free!
I before E, except after C—All of this homework leaves no time to be me!

Suddenly Daniela added:

Also when saying A, like neighbour or weigh.
I know it's cliché—but send this homework away!

Then everyone joined in the chorus:

Big Elephants Can Always Understand Small Elephants. Yeah Yeah Yeah.
Big Elephants Can Always Understand Small Elephants. Yeah Yeah Yeah.

The song sounded pretty cool with all the different harmonies. I could feel my head bobbing up and down despite myself. Still, I wasn't sold on the chorus—especially because it was written by a blackmailer.

"Isn't everyone going to wonder what we're singing about? First we're singing a blues tune about homework, and suddenly we're harmonizing about the heartfelt connection between zoo animals?"

"Actually, I think it adds a cool sense of mystery to the song," said Sludge. "I loved the Perogies' song, 'Filled with Potato and Cheese' because, for the longest time, I didn't know what they were singing about. At first I thought they were saying 'Fight the Tomatoes and Peas.' I thought it was another protest song about that new vegan pasta the caf' experimented with last month. Then, when I actually figured out what they were saying, I thought it was about Mr. Papernick. You know how he's always lecturing us about making the most of our abilities. *Blah, blah, blah.* I thought the Perogies were talking about how he's full of hot air. Not until the caf' held their annual international lunch day did I learn that the Perogies were singing about stuffed dumplings."

"Weren't you *annoyed* when you finally realized

you had it wrong? That they were just singing about *lunch*?" I asked him.

"Not at all," said Sludge smiling. "In my mind, it's still about Papernick. I hum it to myself every time he lectures me about not finishing my homework."

I could see Sludge's point. The grade eights would think the song was a bluesy shout-out to the rough days they had when they'd first arrived as innocent grade sixers—from big fishes at Pleasant Valley Elementary School to nothings at Wilcott. And the grade sixers might think the song was a ballad of friendship from the grade sevens and eights. If all else failed, Wilcotters for the Ethical Treatment of Poor Defenceless Animals could turn it into a song about the sensitivity of elephants. Regardless, I couldn't get the chorus out of my head—a good sign for the upcoming spelling test.

"I guess it's useable if we work on it a bit," I finally said grudgingly. I didn't look at Eldrick as we took our places and began to practice our new song.

$$(^2 / x + -)$$

As much as I hated to admit it, Eldrick's song helped me stay in the band. I hummed my way through the spelling test and got a B-plus. I would have aced the test if I hadn't mixed up dessert and desert. I proudly showed the Z's my spelling test. Later, I found them in the back of the cafeteria, scribbling furiously. Their matching blue and mauve berets bopped up and down as they wrote. Beena waved me over when she saw me.

"We've got something for you," she said.

"A new song," nodded Meena. "We call it 'Second Helping.'"

Beena grabbed her blue harmonica and got them in tune.

> *Dessert, Dessert!*
> *Having two can't hurt.*
> *You'll dream of deuce*
> *If it's chocolate mousse.*
> *You'll always want seconds*
> *When a piece of cherry pie beckons.*
> *Remember that it's two*
> *If it's covered in marshmallow goo…*

"What's this all about?" I finally interrupted.

"We really want you to stay in the band," said Meena.

"So we came up with a way for you to remember how to spell dessert. Double helpings mean double S," continued Beena.

I was happily surprised that the Z's had written me a song about marshmallow glop. Spelling was becoming a breeze. Algebra was another story but, luckily, the next test wasn't until after the District Donnybrook.

Chapter 15

The District Donnybrook was being held at a middle school across town. Meena and Beena's father had rented a van so we could transport all of our gear. Daniela went over to the Z's earlier in the day so they could help with her costume. I was the last pick-up. I entered the van and immediately sensed the nervousness.

"Daniela, did you bring some tea with you?" I asked.

She didn't answer.

"Daniela," I repeated, "did you bring anything to help warm up your throat?"

She still didn't answer.

"Fine," I said, giving in. "*Olaf*, did you bring anything with you?"

"When I'm Olaf, I'm Olaf," explained Daniela to the Z's. To me she replied, "A thermos of warm tea made from imported Scandinavian herbs—a present from Sarah Hibbit."

"Cool. Sludge, you've got all your equipment?"

"Yup," he replied.

"Great. Z's, did you remember your lucky blue and mauve guitar picks?"

The Z's nodded in unison.

"Uh, and you, Hooperberg, do you have your, um..."

I was trying to be a bit nicer to him because he had helped me stay in the band.

"...do you have your triangle wand?"

"Got it!" said Eldrick, beaming.

There was a huge crowd milling around Whitner Middle School when we arrived. We pushed through the crowd and headed to the gymnasium. It was just as chaotic behind the stage. Everyone was jostling to get to a mirror. Some kids were stretching. Others were holding hands and taking deep breaths. There was a mish-mash of voices, both high and low, as a few musical groups went over their songs. Ten acts were slated to compete at the District Donnybrook. We were scheduled to go ninth. Hopefully, Daniela wouldn't get too nervous during the long wait. She was standing by the big, red curtain that kept us hidden from the audience.

"Whatcha doin', Cuz?" I asked her, trying to sound casual.

"There are a lot of people here," she said, gesturing to the big auditorium on the other side. The loud sound of chatter told us the room was packed. I squeezed her hand tightly.

The room went silent when Principal Bording took the stage. Everyone knew about Whitner's principal. He was also known as Principal Boring. His monotonous speeches were legendary, even across town at Wilcott. Joe Jacobs once fell asleep at a basketball game when Principal Boring took twenty minutes to introduce his team. Teammates tried to shake Joe awake but he was snoring soundly. Finally, they threw a glass of water in Joe's face to get him on the court before tip-off.

Principal Boring was just warming up. "I would like to welcome everyone to Whitner Middle School and to the best talent competition in the city. We've got ten acts representing the various schools in the district tonight. The act that receives the loudest cheer will be crowned winner and will go on to compete in the City Championship. Tonight should offer a very respectable evening of music, dancing, camaraderie, and competition. Entertainment is a cornerstone of our society..."

Blah, blah, blah. Somewhere in the auditorium, Joe Jacobs was probably struggling to keep his eyes open. At long last, Principal Boring finally left the stage. Game on!

First up was a one-man band called Me, Myself and I. Me was a great singer, a good piano player, an average guitarist and a truly awful harmonica player. Next up was Style Over Substance, an all-boy band from Farmington Middle School. They took the stage looking awesome in coordinating green-and-blue track suits. They began with some fierce hip-hop moves. Sludge and I exchanged worried glances. We breathed a sigh of relief when they started to sing. They huffed and puffed into their microphones as they tried to keep up with their dancing. Third up was a group called the Equations singing an ode to their principal.

"I guess every school's gotta have one," commented Sludge.

Suddenly, the competition started to heat up.

Heyward Elementary's entry was a contortionist. She received a loud round of applause for twisting her feet behind her head and turning herself into a human pretzel. Two solid dance crews followed.

A girl and boy who claimed to be plate spinners were next. They appeared on stage with four porcelain dishes and four rods. At first I thought they were going to build a campfire and roast marshmallows. Then the girl took the rods and balanced them in her hands. The boy took one of the plates and tossed it in the air. It landed on the girl's rod, spinning away! They did this three more times until all of the plates were spinning in unison. The crowd clapped appreciatively. The girl threw all four plates up in the air and caught them on the rods. And they were still spinning! I had never seen anything like it before. The crowd clapped louder.

It was almost time for Sick on a Snow Day to take the stage. We huddled together and watched the eighth act. It was a ten-piece band called Peanut Butter and Jam that came complete with a banjo, stand-up bass, saxophone, and bongo drums.

"Where's the triangle?" sniffed Eldrick.

PB and J played only one song—"Crunchy or Smooth"—and they sounded tight. Everyone in the audience was on their feet and clapped along. PB and J was our stiffest competition yet. I wanted to give our band a last-minute pep talk but it was impossible to be heard over the deep thump of the bongos.

PB and J wrapped up their performance to a standing ovation. Suddenly, we were about to take centrestage. For the first time, I could feel butterflies in my stomach. I prayed that my sweaty palms wouldn't affect my piano playing. A strange shrieking noise vibrated from the back of the auditorium. We assumed it was feedback from the amplifiers and waited for the sound technician to fix it. But the wailing seemed to get louder. The Z's adjusted their guitars but the noise persisted. I listened more closely. It didn't sound like typical feedback. The shrieking was too...*girly*. I peeked through the curtain and tried to see what was going on. Sure enough, there were Lisa, Sarah, Janine and a gaggle of other Wilcott girls. Decked out in oversized sunglasses, they were pushing their way up to the front of the auditorium. Squinting in the dark, I could see they were holding a banner that read *Olaf's Army*. Their pushing got aggressive as people started to push back. The situation was getting out of hand.

I took a step away from the curtain just as it pulled back and the lights hit us. Sludge quickly counted the beat and we launched into "Detention Blues." The pushing and shrieking stopped. That's when I saw that Daniela wasn't kidding earlier. It was like she'd just *become* Olaf—and he sounded awesome, though it was hard to hear him during the chorus. Olaf's Army had made its way to the front and were joining in:

> *The Detention Blues, oh so blue*
> *And he's also grounded, too.*

Before I knew it, the song was over. It was time for me to introduce our new song. "This is a new one called 'Big Elephants Can Always Understand Small Elephants.' We wrote it a few weeks ago."

Sludge began singing in a falsetto:

> *I before E, except after C—I just need time to be free!*
> *I before E, except after C—All of this homework leaves no time to be me!*

Meena joined in on guitar as Sludge continued the first verse. Then it was Olaf's turn to join. His deep voice provided a contrasting harmony. Soon we were all playing: I was tinkling, Beena was strumming, and Eldrick was chiming. Olaf's Army had recruited every female in the room. They joined in for the chorus:

> *Big Elephants Can Always Understand*
> *Small Elephants. Yeah Yeah Yeah.*
> *Big Elephants Can Always Understand*
> *Small Elephants. Yeah Yeah Yeah.*

Swivelling my head, I caught a glimpse of Eldrick. He was ratcheting, pinging, and shaking his tambourine with gusto. Though I had vowed never to forgive the tattling blackmailer, it was hard not to give in to the moment and smile at him. Instead, I focused on Olaf. He finished the song by kicking his mike stand to the ground like a true rock star.

The room erupted in cheers. Sludge ran out from behind his drum kit. "We rocked it!" he hollered. "Completely, one-hundred percent *rocked* it!"

It was hard to hear him over the pandemonium. Everyone was on their feet. I had expected all of the cheering to come from female voices. But the hooting and hollering was balanced. The entire audience was cheering.

"I think we're ahead of PB and J," whispered my cousin Olaf excitedly as we exited stage left. The twins nodded enthusiastically.

"The last act is a comedian," said Sludge. "How much competition can a dude telling jokes be?"

A very tall girl walked on stage and introduced herself as Helen the Hysterical from Spiller Academy.

"Or a girl," corrected Sludge.

I was anxious to hear her act. Although we had just slayed the room, nothing could top an audience bent over in helpless laughter. I stood at the wings of the stage and listened intently.

"Why did the tomato turn red?" asked Helen.

I leaned in closely to hear the answer…just as Olaf spun me around and began to go over the finer points of his performance. Stuck listening to him reminiscing about his lower register, I missed why the tomato was so rosy. But I did hear the audience giggling. I managed to shake Olaf by telling him the twins wanted to discuss his scissor-kick technique.

"An emu, three hippos, and a clown walk into a pizzeria," started Helen.

This sounded like it could be a doozy. Even from behind the curtain, I could see the audience smiling.

"The emu turns to one of the hippos and says—"

"I have a great idea for a new song," said Sludge, choosing that exact moment to whisper into my ear, "A tune that will totally blow everyone away."

Sheesh! While I admired his confidence, I really wanted to hear what the emu had to say.

But Sludge could not be stopped. He blabbered on and on until I missed not only what the emu said but how the hippos replied. It must have been good because the audience quickly cracked up with laughter.

"I'll leave you with this last one," began Helen.

This time I didn't even get to hear the set up. Eldrick and Sludge decided that now would be the perfect time to go over every instrument an auxiliary percussionist could play.

"Anything you can hit or scrape, basically," said Eldrick. "Like bells or chimes—"

"Awesome," responded Sludge.

"—or a marimba, a xylophone, a glockenspiel—"

"Awesomer," opined Sludge.

"—or a tympani—"

"The most awesomest," decided Sludge.

I gave up trying to listen to Helen's material. It didn't matter anyway—it was impossible to hear the punch line over the audience's roaring laughter.

"Thank you, you've been great tonight," said Helen as she exited the stage. The audience was in stitches. The atmosphere was a mix of giggles and grins.

Principal Bording was smiling from ear to ear when he took the stage. "'It saw the salad dressing!' Classic!" It took him a few moments to stop chortling. But then he cleared his throat and went back to being Principal Boring.

"I would like to give a big thanks to all of our participants tonight." He insisted on thanking every act individually. Butterflies fluttered around my stomach as he went on and on. "I want to congratulate all of our contestants. Me, Myself and I, thank you for showing us the joys of multi-tasking. Looking good, Style Over Substance. Maybe you can show me a few of your moves later. The Equations, you're my personal favourites. And the plate spinners, you can come and unload my dishwasher anytime..."

I was going to explode if he didn't hurry up! He continued until he had nothing else to say—except what we were all waiting for.

"And the winner of this year's District Donnybrook is..."

Olaf cracked his knuckles.

"Sick on a Snow Day!"

Meena and Beena let out matching screams. Olaf pumped his fist over his head. Sludge threw Eldrick into the air. He had a bit of trouble catching him. We tried to compose ourselves as Principal Bording handed us a silver trophy.

"Whoever wrote 'Big Elephants Can Always Understand Small Elephants' is a genius. I love political songs. I wasn't sure if it was about the relationship between Canada and the United States or if it was about big-market sports teams versus teams that play in smaller cities. But I loved it, nonetheless." We tried not to giggle as he hummed the chorus. "Keep writing those deep, meaningful

115

songs and you'll have a real shot at winning the City Championship."

Olaf raised the trophy above his head. Olaf's Army screamed in delight. The audience was still applauding as we left the stage.

Chapter 16

We were greeted like rock stars upon our return to school. Everyone wanted to talk to us. Some kids wanted to hang out and talk music while others just wanted to congratulate us.

"Do I know her?" I asked Daniela (now that she *was* Daniela again) and pointed to a short girl with curly hair who had just hugged me.

"Don't think so," Daniela replied.

"What about that guy?" I asked referring to a tall kid who had just invited me over to his house for dinner.

"No idea who that is," said my cousin.

The school wanted to hold a little party the next day in honour of the band's victory.

"Maybe we'll sign some autographs," said Meena.

"I'm willing to kiss my fans," said Sludge generously.

It sounded like fun! Lisa, Janine, and Sarah

were organizing the festivities. Amazingly, Principal Losman agreed to cancel last period so we could all meet in the gym and celebrate. But first, he insisted on having a meeting with the band.

"He wants to see us during lunch time," said Daniela.

I swore I saw Sludge elbow Eldrick in the ribs.

"We can't make it, man," said Sludge.

"Why not? This is important," I told them.

"We, uh...umm. We, uh..." Sludge fumbled for words.

"I'm tutoring Sludge in geography," said Eldrick.

Something sounded fishy. "You're tutoring a grade eight when you're only in grade six?"

"I'm a land-and-water whiz," offered Eldrick.

Why would Sludge want to spend extra time with that twerp? Something was up, but I didn't have time to get to the bottom of it. Lisa was insisting on going over the party plans.

"We've asked everyone to come dressed in either yellow or blue," she said excitedly. "Isn't that cool?"

"Sure, I guess so," I said reluctantly. My favourite colours were black and green.

"Yellow and blue," she said, eyeing me with exasperation. "The national colours of Sweden. We're going to arrange everyone in the bleachers so we make a human flag. Don't you think Olaf will love that?"

"He'll love it—if he can make it," I told her. She had caught me a bit off guard. "He's got a big report due in Stockholm this week."

Lisa's face crumpled up. "He *has* to come!" she wailed. "The party's in his honour! Sarah! Janine! Olaf might pull a no-show for his own party!"

Janine and Sarah showed up out of nowhere. "What do you mean he won't be there?" They were getting hysterical.

"Okay, okay," I said trying to diffuse the situation. "I'll see what I can do. Maybe he can finish his report tonight."

"He *has* to come," cried Sarah.

"He *is* the band," sniffled Janine. "It's called *Olaf*'s Army, not *Adam*'s Army."

I got her message loud and clear. The awesome

support we got at the District Donnybrook was because of our tall, Swedish, lead singer. Without him, we'd just be another band. I was in a bit of a pickle. Olaf's Army was the key to our success. I had to keep them happy, even if it meant making Daniela hobnob with her fans.

"I'll make sure he's there," I told them.

Daniela was going to kill me!

$$(^2 / x + -)$$

In the end, I was the only one who met with Principal Losman. Sludge and Eldrick had their mysterious tutoring session. Beena and Meena were busy giving an interview to the school newspaper. And Daniela was too furious to speak to anyone.

"I am not going to any stupid party as Olaf," she had huffed when I told her. "I don't speak Swedish and I don't want Janine Stroop hanging off of me." She stomped off angrily. I headed to the office by myself.

Principal Losman led me into his room. "Congratulations on your victory."

"Thanks," I said. "And thanks for letting us celebrate during last period tomorrow."

"That's what I want to talk to you about," said Principal Losman, getting straight to the point.

"Adam," started Prinicpal Losman. His tone made me think of my parents—not a good thing. "Maybe it's time to end this charade. The school is going wild for a student who doesn't even exist. I think it's becoming too much."

Janine's words, "*It's called Olaf's Army, not Adam's Army,*" echoed in my mind. I knew what would happen if our hoax was revealed.

"Please, Principal Losman," I begged, "let Sick on a Snow Day compete in the City Championship with Olaf as lead singer. I know I promised you he would be 33,000 feet in the air right now, but I never expected to make it this far. Daniela still needs him. Our band still needs him. The whole school is supporting our group, and Olaf is the star attraction. Please let us take the final step. We've worked so hard—all of us. And nothing's ever meant more to me." And I meant it.

Principal Losman looked thoughtful for a

moment. "In the nine months that I've known you, Adam, you've been in my office quite a few times. I have to say, it's nice to see you getting involved in an *appropriate* school activity. Your teachers are still concerned about your tendency to daydream in class, but so far, your marks are holding steady. And, albeit in a strange way, you're demonstrating some fine leadership skills." He took a deep breath.

"School spirit has definitely been high over the past few weeks, too. That's certainly worth something. So, let's play it by ear for the next little while. Olaf is welcome to appear at the rally tomorrow—but then you'll need to send him off on a field trip for a few days."

"Thanks, Principal Losman," I said as he shook my hand. "We'll keep everything under control. I promise!"

So, Olaf's invitation was extended! Now I just had to figure out what to do about the assembly. And Daniela.

Chapter 17

It was party time! The gym was packed when we arrived. Since we were being treated like rock stars, we decided to act like rock stars. Instead of going through the front doors, we snuck through the back and took the stage. The curtain was drawn. Had it been open, all of Wilcott would have seen that we were ready to rock. It was Eldrick's idea to treat the school to a quick set of songs. As much as I hated to admit it, it was a great idea: It gave Olaf maximum separation from his adoring fans and made it easier for us to keep up our end of the bargain with Principal Losman. Olaf could appear onstage and sing, but then he had to disappear. Even Daniela was convinced that the plan was solid, so she had agreed to perform.

On cue, the room went black. Meena drew back the curtains and picked up her guitar. Olaf grabbed the mike and the crowd went crazy. Daniela was worried about being recognized so Olaf was wearing his signature over-sized shades and a funky scarf. Beena had wound the scarf so far up his neck that it covered his chin. Combined with the huge sunglasses, it made an effective disguise. We breezed through "Detention Blues."

I knew Lisa planned to present Olaf with flowers after the show. But I was ready to foil her plan. We launched into "Big Elephants Can Always Understand Small Elephants." Olaf sounded great. He got to the final chorus and belted it out: *Big Elephants Can Always Understand Small Elephants. Yeah Yeah Yeah...*

Suddenly, the curtain was drawn again. When it opened again, Sick on a Snow Day was a five-piece orchestra. Olaf was nowhere to be seen.

Lisa approached the stage with a big bouquet of flowers. Confused, she looked around the stage. She climbed over Sludge's drum kit and under my keyboard. But her search turned up empty. Olaf had left the building.

"Where is he?" she whined.

"I'm sorry," I said into the microphone so the whole school could hear, "but Olaf has an appointment for a Swedish massage and sauna."

A big sigh of disappointment travelled through the room. I cleared my throat to get everyone's attention. "He said to tell you he was sorry, but it's very important that Swedish rock stars have massages and saunas to keep them in good rocking condition. He says he'll see you at the City Championship. *Go Wilcott!*"

Just mentioning the final talent competition brightened the mood of the room.

"We had a special surprise for Olaf," said a visibly disappointed Lisa. "We'll just have to give it to the rest of the band. Sarah, unveil the table."

At the back of the room, Sarah pulled a sheet off a long table. I couldn't see what was on the table but I could tell from the gasps of my classmates that whatever sat there wasn't anything normally found at J.R. Wilcott. Sludge, Eldrick, the twins, and I gingerly made our way to the table. There sat some of the strangest-looking things I had ever seen. I thought it was food but I wasn't one-hundred percent sure.

"Ugh, take a whiff," said Sludge holding his nose.

Something on the table smelled revolting. Like a gross mixture of dirty diapers and smelly socks. I looked at Sludge. He looked terrified. Lisa and Sarah, on the other hand, looked delighted.

"We thought Olaf might be a bit homesick," said Lisa smiling. "So we surfed the internet to find out what foods are popular in Sweden. Our plan was to surprise him with a buffet of his favourite food. A smorgasbord—just like at home!"

"What, uh, is this stuff?" I said, trying not to gag. I did my best not to breathe through my nose.

She pointed to a grey, fishy-looking thing that sat on a limp piece of dark brown bread. It looked raw. "Herring on rye—Stockholm style!" We must have looked clueless, because she continued her explanation. "Salted fish with onions, served on a lard spread."

Eww!

Beside that was a mushy, brown concoction sprinkled with red blotches. "Liver pate with red beets."

No explanation needed there! The last item on the table was the one stinking up the room. To my eye, it looked like cheese but, with a stench like that, I wasn't positive. The only cheese I ate came with macaroni. The room fell silent as Janine introduced the mystery item.

"We read that they eat a lot of old, smelly cheeses in Sweden, so we got the stinkiest one we could find: finely-aged Limburger." She sounded very proud of herself.

"Well?" said Lisa as she looked directly at me. I glanced nervously at Sludge for support.

"He *is* your cousin," said Janine. Worried, I looked at the twins for help.

Sarah was direct. "We went through all this trouble for Olaf and he's not here. Someone's got to try the smorgasbord...and since you're the one who's related to him, it might as well be you." I tried desperately to make eye-contact with Eldrick. "Dig in," said Sarah handing me a piece of slimy herring.

All of Wilcott was silently watching me. I swallowed hard and forced a tight smile. It was important I keep Olaf's Army happy—at least until the City Championship was over. Janine, Sarah and Lisa would be insulted if I didn't sample their hard work. I was backed into a corner—a disgustingly smelly corner! The rest of Sick on a Snow Day looked on helplessly. I glanced at the herring in my hand. A purple onion dangled limply from its side. Closing my eyes, I put the fish in my mouth. I put it as far back on my tongue as it would go. My grand plan was to eat the slithery fish without chewing it. One huge gulp later, the herring was gone.

Sludge gave me a pat on the back. "One down, two to go. You can do it!" he whispered in encouragement.

Next up was the liver and beets. Quickly, I slid it down my throat before it had a chance to infiltrate my taste buds. Done! Disgusting but done!

The final act was now: the super-smelly, nasty Limburger cheese. I was up to the challenge of slimy herring and mushy liver, but stinky cheese was another story. I wasn't a big fan of cheese. I rarely ate the stuff, even when it was the non-smelly, boring, yellow kind. I cut myself a little piece. My eyes started to water from the smell. But I continued. Sick on a Snow Day was worth a mouthful of grossness. Slowly, I brought the stink bomb of cheese to my lips. I caught another whiff and started to feel dizzy. I wanted to go through with it, but my mouth wouldn't open.

Suddenly, a cold hand grabbed the cheese away from me.

"I love smelly cheese," said a high-pitched voice. "It would be my honour to sample the Limburger."

It was Eldrick. He was saving me! I rubbed my eyes into focus and looked at him. Eldrick didn't look like he loved Limburger cheese. In fact, he looked a little green. But, standing as tall as he could, he brought the stinky stuff to his mouth. And then he ate it. Coughing and gagging, Eldrick tried his best not spit the Limburger out on Janine's shoes. Thinking quickly, Sludge handed him a bottle of juice. Eldrick downed the whole bottle and then stood up straight.

The room burst into applause. "Speech! Speech!" demanded the crowd.

Eldrick did not look up to giving a speech. I grabbed the microphone instead.

"A big thanks to everyone for showing up for this great party," I started. "It's great to have everyone's support. I want to thank Janine, Lisa and

Sarah for going through all the trouble of creating a traditional Swedish smorgasbord. I can't wait to see the look on Olaf's face when I show him all these, er, *delicious* leftovers."

I also needed to thank someone else important—the guy who saved me from the killer cheese—but I would do that privately after school. For now, I just gave Eldrick a smile. I knew what he had done for me. And after he finished his fourth bottle of juice, he smiled back.

Chapter 18

The City Championship was right around the corner and Sick on a Snow Day was ready. Daniela was feeling comfortable and confident as "Olaf." And Eldrick and I were getting along very well. He was full of helpful tips. He suggested that Sludge add a bongo drum to his percussion kit. The two of them spent hours picking out the perfect bongo.

His study tips kept me in the band. For some strange reason, Eldrick seemed to take quite an interest in my grades—and I couldn't complain. With the exception of math, I was breezing through all of my tests and assignments. He was always careful to offer suggestions to the whole band, but we all knew whose musical fate depended on a B-average. Mine!

"HOMES," he told us one day. "HOMES is the key to the geography test. Each letter stands for one of the Great Lakes."

Today, Eldrick came to practice spouting nonsense. "Mary Very Easily Makes Jam Saturday Unless No Plums."

"A new song?" asked Daniela.

He kept repeating the gobbledy-gook until we were all chanting the nonsense.

"Great," he told me after practice. "Now you know all of the planets. Mars, Venus, Earth, Mercury, Jupiter, Saturn, Uranus, Neptune, Pluto. You'll ace the science test.

"I thought Pluto's not a planet anymore," piped up Sludge. "Heard it got downgraded to a dwarf planet or something."

"True, Sludge, but—" started Eldrick.

I interrupted before Eldrick could respond to Sludge. The study tips were great and all, but we had a city championship to win. We needed to forget about the Milky Way and focus on music.

"I've been working on a new song!" I told everyone. "I think it's got potential. It's dark and moody." I played a simple intro on the piano.

Attacked by a herring while everyone was staring
Choking back mushy liver as I try not to quiver
Oh taste buds, can you forgive?
No more slimy fish for as long as I live...

"That's all I've got so far," I told my friends.

"Very dark, very moody," agreed Daniela.

"I wrote a new song, too," said Sludge. He played us a few bars of "To Ink or Not to Ink."

"It's a look into the world of tattoos," he explained.

Every member of Sick on a Snow Day wanted to write the song that would win the City Championship. Next up were the Z's who had written a bouncy number about being identical twins called "Joined at the Hip."

"Time for my song," said Eldrick cheerfully. "I haven't given it a title yet."

Sludge was the best songwriter in the band but Eldrick was proving to be a close second. Being nerdy, he had a huge vocabulary and a way with words. Though his speaking voice was high and squeaky, his singing voice was surprisingly deep.

It's night time and there you are lying awake—
Tomorrow you are going to make a giant mistake

> *Sometimes it's hard to face the terrors*
> *Of a test filled with red-marked errors*

Something about this song was starting to bug me.

> *He was going to cheat on the test he*
> *wanted to ace*
> *But in the end, he couldn't go through*
> *with the disgrace*

Eldrick was singing about me! Sludge and the Z's had also figured it out. They looked nervous as he sang the chorus:

> *Let me suggest (la la la)*
> *How you can ace the test (la la la)*
> *Don't let yourself go astray (la la la)*
> *Just so you can get an A (la la la)—*

"That's ENOUGH!!" I exploded.

"Wait!" protested Eldrick. "You haven't heard the whole thing yet! Wait until you hear the rest!"

Daniela spoke gently but firmly. "Eldrick, why would Adam want to hear a song about how he got into so much trouble—especially from the guy who got him into the trouble?"

"I uh, I...it wasn't my....I didn't mean..." he blustered. "But there's no cheating—"

I'd heard enough. "I thought we were finally friends! You ate stinky cheese for me! And now you want to sing this and embarrass me in front of the whole city? Some friend."

"I...I...it wasn't to embarrass you, Adam," whispered Eldrick. Near tears, he fumbled to explain himself. "I...uh...tried...meaningful lyrics. Just let me finish."

"Eldrick," Daniela interrupted gently. "I think you've sung enough for now."

We all stood in an awkward silence. I refused to look at Eldrick.

"I guess you want me to leave?" he asked dully.

"I'll say we do," I fumed. The rest of the band stood there mutely.

"What are we going to do?" asked Daniela when he was finally gone.

It was a tough decision. On the one hand, we didn't want to mess with a winning formula. Eldrick was a good songwriter and a top-notch percussionist. On the other hand, just when I thought we had made peace, he'd tried to humiliate me again.

"My vote is to kick him out," I said. I knew

I sounded harsh, but I was still smarting over his song. My cheeks were burning with embarrassment.

"What he did was pretty dumb," said Beena, "but he does come up with ways for you to pass your tests. Are you sure you want to kick him out so close to the City Championship?"

Sludge had an idea. "Can we give him some sort of detention for screwing up?" He had a lot of experience in detentions. "Something like a detention suspension?"

"Good idea," said Daniela, "We can suspend him for a few practices and then bring him back for the City Championship."

After taking a vote, we decided to suspend Eldrick for three practices. I had pushed for ten but the rest of the band talked me out of it.

"We don't have ten practices before the contest," pointed out the twins.

Daniela went to break the news to Eldrick. The whole episode put me in a bad mood.

"Use your negative energy, dude," said Sludge.

I grabbed a pen and paper, hoping to churn out a dark but catchy song.

Chapter 19

The timing couldn't have been worse for Eldrick's suspension. Mr. Papernick set the big algebra test for the day before the City Championship. I tried to talk him out of it.

"Can't you make it the day after?" I begged.

Mr. Papernick wouldn't budge. And he wasn't moved by my offer to dedicate our next song to him.

My parents had the same reaction. "You need to get a B on the test. Rules are rules."

"Even though the City Championship is the next day?" I asked.

"*Especially* because the championship is the next day. This will help you learn how to manage your time and focus on what's important."

Time management and focusing? Sometimes my parents spoke in a strange language. I knew what was important to me. The City Championship had a cash prize.

"I have the chance to win a thousand dollars and

buy you something really nice," I told my mother.

She gave me her special look: a combination of "stop pushing your luck" and "I've had enough." Although my brother, Josh, had been given this look before, it was my first time. I slunk out of the room without saying another word.

"How can they expect me to concentrate on a math test when the biggest day of my life is right around the corner?" I complained to Daniela.

"Maybe you can write a song about it?" she suggested. "Call it 'Full Circle.' You got into this mess because you focused only on the band and ignored a math test and now you desperately need to ace a math test to stay in the band."

"I think it's so unfair," I said, ignoring her. "I've done everything they asked. I can spell *dessert*. I can spell *desert*. I know the difference between *principle* and *principal*. They know math is my weakness. Order of operations? Ugh! What am I going to do?"

"Aside from studying?" asked Daniela.

My cousin was really irritating me today. "How can I study when I'm trying to write us a championship song?"

"I have an idea," said Daniela, "but you're going to hate it."

"Fire away," I said, defeated.

"Cut Eldrick's suspension detention."

"Right," I said sarcastically, "like that will help me manage my time and focus."

Daniela had had enough of my tone. "No, dummy. He won't help you focus on the test, but he will help you *pass* the test. So far, he's helped you pass every spelling, science, and history test."

"You might have a point," I conceded reluctantly. "But I have my *principles*!"

"Principles-shminciples," said Daniela. "Who taught you how to spell the word?"

"He didn't teach me how to spell the word," I said stubbornly. "He just taught me a lame rhyme about Principal Losman being my *pal*."

"He taught you how to spell the word," said Daniela firmly. "He's already served almost all of his suspension. Just call him and invite him back early."

I was close to caving. But then I remembered his song and stubbornly refused.

"Then go and study!" ordered Daniela.

It wasn't as easy as that. Sick on a Snow Day was the first act in J.R. Wilcott's history to compete in the City Championship. There were a lot of demands on our time. Our local newspaper, the *Gazette*, wanted to interview us before the competition. We also had a photo shoot. I was just too busy to study.

And, of course, the City Championship provided a zillion daydreaming opportunities. Staring out the window and thinking about holding that winner's cheque was way more interesting than going through my math book. It was no contest. Studying was next to impossible.

Chapter 20

Everything in my life was going at full speed. School, the City Championship, tricking the school into thinking I had a cute, Swedish cousin: It was too much. The algebra test was the next day. The band knew I was in trouble, but tried to pretend everything was okay.

We had just finished practicing a new song in our repertoire. It was another one of Sludge's masterpieces.

"Have you given a copy of the music to Eldrick?" asked Daniela. "He needs a chance to rehearse, too."

"Don't worry about it. I went by his place a few days ago and we went over the song. He knows it inside and out!" Sludge enthused. "The little guy can play everyone's part. And I mean *everyone's* part," he added carefully.

"That was a good idea," said Beena.

"Really good," sighed Meena.

"I hope you understand," Sludge said

uncomfortably. "I just thought we should have our bases covered. Just in case..."

I nodded wordlessly. The thought of being out of Sick on a Snow Day made me slightly sick, myself. But I understood. A shadow was cast over the room. Everyone knew math was my weakest subject. Daniela nervously twisted her blond wig.

"Let's not get all doom-and-gloom just yet," suggested Beena. "How bad can it be?"

"I've tried studying every night," I told them. "But, you know what? It just seems like if it's not one of our songs, it's not sticking in my head. I've gone over the chapter ten times, but it's just not working. These days, the only notes in my head are *musical* notes. I don't have room for anything else."

"Study hard tonight and maybe you'll pull it off," said Sludge half-heartedly.

The Z's nodded dejectedly. I tried to smile but my face felt frozen. Beside me was the math text book. It looked three times bigger than it had a few minutes ago. I blinked and looked again. Somehow it had gotten even bigger! I forced myself to look away.

I looked Daniela in the eye. "I'm desperate. I'll give anything a shot."

She knew what I meant. "Eldrick. Let's call him and see if he can help."

Minutes later, there was a soft knock on the door and Eldrick appeared. I was pretty sure Eldrick lived on the other side of the block. He must have sprinted to get here so quickly.

"Wow. You were pretty speedy," I marvelled. I wasn't sure, but I thought I saw a look pass among my bandmates.

"So, the test is on chapter thirteen," said Eldrick shyly, but jumping right in. "You need to know how to handle equations. What do you do when you have a bunch of numbers and a bunch of signs between them? Do you divide first? Or do you multiply? What about brackets?"

"I don't know," I said dejectedly. "If I knew, I wouldn't need you."

"You need to figure out what to do first. Technically, it's called order of operations. But we call it BEDMAS."

"BEDMAS?" I repeated. That sounded vaguely familiar. Now I remembered Mr. Papernick mentioning it last week when I was busy trying to write some new lyrics. I couldn't figure out why he was talking about sloppy bedrooms.

"Brackets, Exponents, Division, Multiplication, Addition, Subtraction. Everything you need to know in the order you need to know it to ace the test," said Eldrick with more confidence.

"Sure," I said doubtfully. "Now I just need to remember all of that."

Suddenly Sludge jumped up. "Got it!" he hollered as he accidentally knocked over a drum. "I've got it! The BEDMAS Conspiracy. That's how you'll remember it!"

"I like it," smiled Eldrick. "A lot."

I was annoyed that Eldrick knew what Sludge was talking about and I didn't.

"The BEDMAS Conspiracy. Our new name," said Sludge. "Don't say no until I explain," he added hastily, looking at the frown on my face. "If it's the name of our band, there's no way you can forget it." I couldn't argue with that.

"But won't people wonder why we suddenly changed our name?" I asked him.

"Nah, they'll be too busy wondering what the

conspiracy actually is!" laughed Sludge. "And little will they know," said Sludge lowering his voice to a whisper, "that it also stands for Beena, Eldrick, Daniela, Meena, Adam and Sludge!"

"I love it," said Meena

"Totally," agreed Beena.

I had to admit that the name sounded cool. And it would definitely help with the math test.

"I guess the BEDMAS Conspiracy should get down to work," I finally agreed. "We need a new song for the championships. Let's get cracking."

"Correction, Cuz. The BEDMAS Conspiracy is definitely going to get cracking—but we'll be dealing with math instead of music, right Eldrick?"

"Definitely," Eldrick answered, more firmly than I might have expected. "Remembering the trick is one thing; applying it is another thing altogether. It's like music—you've got to practice it."

The rest of the group looked equally determined.

"Just think of it as a side project," said Sludge, grinning. "We're a band, after all."

I opened my mouth to argue but then I realized—

they were right. All I had to do was get past this one, last test. And I didn't want to let my band down.

"Fine," I conceded at last. "Pass me a pencil."

Chapter 21

It was the morning of the test. Butterflies flitted around my stomach. The BEDMAS Conspiracy gave me confidence. My family didn't.

"I can fill in for you at the City Championship if you flame out today," joked Josh.

"Not funny," I glared.

"Enough," warned my mom. "Adam needs your support if he's going to get a B in his worst subject."

I wished they would all be quiet!

The Z's were waiting for me at my locker.

"Remember: The BEDMAS Conspiracy," they said together.

Beena handed me a blue pencil. "My good-luck pencil. Use it."

Eldrick was also hanging around my locker. He seemed unsure if he was in my good books or my bad ones.

"You'll do fine," he said as we walked into the classroom.

Mr. Papernick ordered us to be quiet and then handed out the test. The hour went by in a blur— just like it had when I first got myself into this mess. But this time I knew what I was doing. Mumbling, "The BEDMAS Conspiracy" to myself I tackled each problem. Brackets, Exponents, Division, Multiplication, Addition, and then Subtraction. I looked over at Eldrick. He was also talking to himself. I gained confidence as I worked through each page. The BEDMAS Conspiracy: Beena, Eldrick, Daniela, Meena, Adam, and Sludge. All my friends, rooting for me.

I flipped to the final page, feeling dizzy with excitement. I was done! The bell rang. The rest of the band was waiting for me at my locker.

"How'd it go, Cuz?" asked Daniela.

"I think I did okay. I wish I didn't have to wait to find out."

"Let's not," said Sludge.

He grabbed my shoulders and pushed me back into the classroom. Daniela, Eldrick, and the Z's followed.

"Mr. P., can you do us a favour and mark Adam's

test right now?" he asked politely. "Our guy really needs to know if he's still in the band."

Mr. Papernick saw the worry on my face. I thought I did well, but I never knew when it came to numbers. He sifted through the stack of tests and removed mine. We hovered around him as he took the lid off his red pen. Right. Right. Wrong. Right. Right. Wrong. His fingers flew as he marked my paper full of checks and crosses. I couldn't watch. I covered my face with my hands. I could hear the Z's gasp, let out a little cheer, and then another gasp. The wait seemed forever.

"Done," he finally said.

Moving my index fingers away from my eye, I gave myself a sliver of sight. All I could see was white. Teeth! Mr. Papernick was smiling. I moved a few more fingers. Sludge was smiling. So were Daniela, Eldrick, and the Z's. I grabbed my test. It was a B with the good type of decorations— a B+!

"*Whoo hoo*," I yelled, punching my fist in the air. "*Whoo hoo!*"

"Yes!" bellowed Sludge.

Daniela and the Z's hugged. Eldrick stood behind them, smiling shyly.

"Time for the BEDMAS Conspiracy to celebrate!" I announced to the rest of the band. "Ice cream and pizza on me!" I grabbed my jacket and bag. Nothing was going to stop me today!

"Adam," laughed Daniela. "It's 10 a.m. We've still got history, English, geography and music."

"Okay, after school. Meet me at my locker. *All* of us," I said, looking directly at Eldrick.

I gave one more whopping *whoo hoo* before heading off to class. Today was amazing!

$$(^2 / x + -)$$

I was still full of *whoo hoos* when we met after school. The pizza place was just a few blocks away. I found myself walking two steps behind everyone else with Eldrick. Not that I was upset. Today was a great day and I knew how to make it even better.

"I just want to say thanks for helping," I told him. "I'm not sure I would have passed this test—all of the tests—without your help."

He frowned, "This mess was my fault in the first place—"

"No, it's my fault, Eldrick. I was the one who made a cheat sheet in the first place," I admitted. "If I hadn't made one, you wouldn't have picked it up off the floor."

Eldrick looked serious. "It's just..." he stopped and tried to find the right words. "I...I just get really nervous sometimes and dumb things come out of my mouth. It happened when I picked up the cheat sheet and it happened again when I wrote that stupid song."

He reached into his pocket and pulled out a crumpled sheet of paper. "I've been carrying this around ever since."

It was the song. He handed it to me. "Please, just read it. The whole thing."

I took the paper and read his lyrics. Once I got through the first few lines, I realized that it wasn't half bad. Yes, it started out about cheating, but then it got better. The song was actually about us—the band. All of us were mentioned. Actually, the lyrics were kind of funny. He had even managed to find a rhyme in *new friends* and *tattoo trends*.

"I didn't mean to embarrass you with the song, Adam. I just wanted to write something great...but, the harder I try, the more I seem to mess up."

For once I really looked at him—this scrawny little guy who everyone thought was a transfer student. His glasses were crooked. His pants were hitched too high and he wore old-man shoes.

But he had helped me stay in the band. He was a pretty good song-writer and a serious musician. And I couldn't forget about the Swedish smorgasbord.

"Any guy who eats stinky cheese for me—without barfing on Janine Stroop's shoes—can't be a total mess-up," I told him smiling. "Let's go celebrate."

Chapter 22

The City Championship was being held at Pleasant Bay School. We planned to meet there an hour before the competition, but Daniela was running late. She couldn't find her wig. My mom helped her search. I was just about to join them in turning Daniela's room upside down, when Abigail came running to the room.

"Finished!" she announced. She presented Daniela's wig—glossy and smooth.

"I washed and conditioned it for you," said Abigail proudly. "I used a special deep conditioner to really make it shine."

"It smells like lilacs," smiled Daniela. "Thanks, Abigail."

"Let's go!" yelled Josh from the landing of the stairs.

We piled into the car. Josh went through a checklist.

"Keyboard?"

"Check."

"Amplifier?"

"Check."

"Wig?"

"Check," said Olaf patting his head.

We were feeling nervous. My mouth was too dry to say much of anything. Olaf's hands were shaking. I grabbed them tightly. My dad concentrated on not getting lost. Sludge was waiting for us in the Pleasant Bay parking lot.

"Hey," he greeted us. "I've been doing a little recon and things are looking good. Everyone's read the article about us in the *Gazette*. The BEDMAS Conspiracy is considered the act to beat tonight."

Hearing that we were front-runners made me more nervous. There were eight acts in the City Championship—one to represent each district in the city. We had to draw our starting position from a hat. I just hoped we didn't have to go first. Olaf was the first to draw. Hands shaking, he reached into the hat and drew the eighth spot.

"Saving the best for last," crowed Sludge. "It doesn't get more awesome than this!"

Unlike Wilcott's Got Talent and the District Donnybrook, the City Championship had judges. It was still the audience who decided the ultimate winner, but three judges sat on a panel, offering feedback after each act.

Eldrick, the Z's, Sludge, Olaf, and I huddled together offstage to watch the competition unfold. The show started with a little presentation from last year's winner, a rock band called No Looking Back. They didn't seem all that happy to be back at the City Championship, but they managed to play a song and tell everyone how they had spent their prize money.

"Buying a ticket out of this town," mumbled their lead singer. The rest of the band nodded.

It was show time! First up was an acrobatic dance pack from McKelvin Middle School. Their name was Flying High, and it fit them perfectly. They flew through the air, doing backflips and handsprings. When they weren't airbound, they tumbled around the stage in perfect unison. The judges loved Flying High and they got a standing ovation.

Next up was Metal Mouth: A Tribute to Braces. The judges put cotton balls in their ears. Metal

Mouth played loud and fast. Their song, "Don't Call Me Brace Face," was a killer.

"Dude, they play with passion," said Sludge with admiration.

Surprisingly, Metal Mouth's second offering was a ballad. Although "The Teeth That Lie Beneath" was sung in barely more than a whisper, it managed to silence the crowd.

"Those are some *personal* lyrics," said Olaf, awestruck.

It was the first thing he had said in over an hour—a good sign that he hadn't gone hoarse with fear. Metal Mouth finished their set by rocking the house with "You'll Be Sorry When They're Off in Nine Months." Though the judges weren't won over, Metal Mouth also received a standing ovation. They dropped their instruments and ran to the front of the stage. Grabbing hands, they took and bow and flashed their metallic grins.

Metal Mouth was followed by a ventriloquist named Barry. He came out on stage with a wooden doll named Harry. Barry sat on a chair. Harry sat on his knee. Harry began to tell a few jokes. The jokes themselves weren't so impressive, but the fact that Barry's lips were drawn as tight as a pencil was. Later, Harry sang a song—while Barry drank a glass of milk! Barry and Harry made a good pair.

Two hip-hop dance crews and a classical pianist followed Barry and his wooden sidekick. They received good feedback from the judges and had the crowd on their feet.

"Everyone is killing it tonight," marvelled Sludge.

"Next up is a hypnotist," said Eldrick. "I bet he turns someone into a monkey."

A gangly guy carrying a large pocket watch took the stage.

"I'm Gary and I go to Jackson Prep," he told the audience.

"I bet he's good," whispered Daniela. The kids who went to the private school were known to be fiercely competitive.

He was *very* good. First, Gary turned a gym teacher into an opera singer. Next, he turned two teenagers into little babies. All it took was a few swings of the watch and *presto*—both kids were crawling on their knees and cooing. One of them stopped to suck his thumb. The audience ate it up!

"Now I'm going to choose someone in the audience and turn them into a farm animal," announced Gary confidently. A hundred arms shot up in the audience. A murmuring of *pick me* travelled through the crowd.

"Huh," said Eldrick. "I never knew so many people were interested in experiencing the life of a cow or pig."

"Who should I pick?" mused Gary as he scanned the audience. He seemed to have difficulty choosing a volunteer, even though he had the whole room to choose from. Suddenly he looked off stage—right at Sludge.

"Hey, how about you?" he asked our drummer.

Sludge looked surprised. "Not the best timing, man," he told Gary.

"It will just take five minutes," said Gary. He looked at the audience. "Clap your hands if you want me to turn Sludge into poultry."

The audience began to clap. It was hard to tell if they were chanting "Sludge" or "McNuggets."

"Just don't turn me into someone's dinner," Sludge told Gary.

"This should be funny," said Beena.

"Strange that he knew Sludge's name," remarked Meena.

Gary made Sludge sit in a chair. He demanded that Sludge keep his eyes on the pocket watch which he swung in front of Sludge's face.

"You are going to get very sleepy," commanded Gary. "And when you wake up, you're going to think you are a chicken."

Sludge's eyes drooped and then closed. Gary clapped his hands and Sludge's eyes flipped open. Sludge took a few tentative steps. He didn't say anything. We all waited silently to see what was going to happen. Suddenly, he bent his arms at the elbow and put his hands under his arms. Then he let out a long *cluuuck*.

"*Cluck, cluck, cluck*," called Sludge as he strutted around the stage.

Gary looked proud of himself and with good reason. Sludge looked hilarious and the audience was eating it up. Sludge started pecking at Gary's hand.

"Here you go, my poultry pal," said Gary as he offered Sludge some sunflower seeds.

"*Cluck, cluck!*" responded Sludge.

The room roared in approval. In spite of my nerves, even I couldn't stop grinning. Sludge strutted to and fro as he continued to cluck.

"Thanks, ladies and gentlemen! You've been a great audience. Enjoy the rest of the show!" Gary bowed and waved to the cheering crowd as it leapt to its feet. Then he led Sludge offstage.

"Thanks for your help, guys," said Gary, grinning. "See you after the show."

"Um, aren't you forgetting something?" Eldrick pointed at Sludge who was preening behind the curtain.

"Oh, right," Gary answered. He turned to Sludge and waved his arms around. "Wake up! Wake up!"

Sludge strutted over. "*Squawk?*" He flapped his "wings" a few times.

"Gee, that's weird." Gary shrugged. "Oh well, I'm sure he'll snap out of it. Let me know how that works out for you." He started down the backstage stairs.

"Hey!" I ran after him in a panic. "Hey, you've got to change him back! Quit fooling around—we're on next!"

"I guess I just don't remember the release code word," Gary said with a tinge of amusement in his voice. "I'm sure it will come to me...eventually."

"You did this on purpose!" I shouted.

"Can't prove anything," smirked Gary. "Except for the fact that I just got the biggest cheer of the night!" It was hard to hear Gary over the loud clucking noise behind me. Sludge had followed us and was pecking Gary's hand again in search of a snack.

"Good luck getting your barnyard buddy to play the drums tonight," sneered Gary as he walked off to join the crowd. Sludge trailed after him.

"What are we going to do?" asked Meena.

"We're next and Sludge is in no shape to drum," said Beena.

"We'll just have to go on without him," I said. It was our only option.

"How can we play without a drummer?" asked Olaf, frowning. "He keeps the beat. He keeps us in time. He *rocks*. We're useless without him."

"I...I...I think I can take over for Sludge," said Eldrick. He looked nervous. "Sludge and I have been working on the whole percussion thing together. I know the songs—and I *am* the auxiliary percussionist. That means drums, too. I think I can do it."

So that's where the two of them had been running off to!

Sludge hopped over to Eldrick and pecked his hand. "I *know* I can do it," said Eldrick gaining confidence.

We were running out of time. The crowd was starting to get restless.

"You're sure you can do it?" asked Daniela.

"Positive," said Eldrick, twirling a drumstick between his fingers.

And somehow, I just knew he was right.

"Then here we go!" I yelled as I led the BEDMAS Conspiracy onto stage: Beena Zellerpin on bass; Meena Zellerpin on lead guitar; Adam Margols on the keyboard; Olaf Danielson (to the squeals of Lisa, Janine, Sarah and every other grade six, seven and eight girl sitting in the front row) on lead vocals; and Eldrick Hooperberg holding down the beat.

For a moment, time seemed to stand still—this was it! Then I heard Eldrick counting us in on "Detention Blues." Olaf began to sing. Beena and Meena began to strum. I carefully tapped the keys in front of me. And Eldrick carried the beat *and* the band. He was fantastic! Olaf sang confidently; the Z's were perfectly in sync; I stopped looking at my fingers just long enough to smile at the audience.

I could see Sludge in the front row. He'd found Gary and was pecking insistently at his shoulder. I wasn't sure if he was exacting revenge or if he'd decided that Gary was the farmer responsible for feeding him. Either way, Gary seemed to be growing increasingly alarmed.

Without pausing between numbers, we moved on to "Big Elephants Can Always Understand Small Elephants." Eldrick sped up the introduction. We managed to keep up with him and the result was awesome. I sneaked a peek at Gary who had his hands full fending off Sludge. It seemed that the music was really riling our former drummer. Not only was he clucking and pecking, but he was batting Gary about the face with his "wings."

Olaf introduced our final number. We had all written it shortly after we adopted our new name, and we had spent hours practicing it.

"It's a song that means a lot to us. It's called 'Unexpected Surprises.'"

Olaf's voice rang out soulfully into the suddenly hushed auditorium, accompanied by a few gentle chords:

> *It's night time and you are lying there awake*
> *Knowing you are about to make a giant mistake*
> *Or suddenly you are so swallowed up by fear*
> *You can't rock the stage and start your singing career.*
>
> *Let me suggest la la la*
> *How you can ace the test la la la*
>
> *Let me suggest la la la*
> *How to be at your best la la la*

Then he kicked the air as the music swelled and the rest of the band came crashing into the chorus:

Sometimes things aren't always what you see,
Surprises where you don't expect them to be.

Olaf's Army was going crazy, shrieking and dancing with their hands in the air. I grinned at Eldrick as he pounded away on the drums.

A friend can be hidden in an old enemy
A simple disguise can hold a new identity.
Did you know sour lemons can make a
sweet drink?
Yeah, they can be squeezed into
lemonade, yellow or pink.

Sometimes things aren't always what you see,
Surprises where you don't expect them to be.

Olaf danced as he sang. He twisted his arms around his head like he was braiding the sky. It looked cool—until he accidentally brushed his left hand up against his wig! I tried not to panic when a strip of bright red hair appeared over his ear. Olaf didn't notice a thing. He was completely involved in his performance.

Refusing to throw in the towel
When your drummer is turned into
a fowl.

He was changing the lyrics! I looked at Beena, who looked at Meena who looked at Eldrick. We hoped Olaf knew what he was doing.

> *You never know what someone can*
> *become—*
> *Scrawny and quiet—but a wizard on*
> *a drum.*

Eldrick launched into his solo and Olaf started to dance wildly. He scissor-kicked the air. The red patch on his head got bigger! He shimmied and shook—and a whole clump of hair spilled down the back of his neck!

Eldrick's solo was over. Everyone joined back in except me. I was too busy using my arms to wave to Olaf. The crowd sang along as he launched into the chorus again.

> *Sometimes things aren't always what you see,*
> *Surprises where you don't expect them to be.*

And then it happened. Olaf gave one last head bob—and we all saw his blond wig go flying. Olaf had left the building!

Exposed, Daniela gasped in shock. Beena and

Meena froze at the same time, their guitar picks poised motionless over the strings. The audience was still on their feet, but the clapping had stopped. The whole room stood in silence staring at my red-headed, un-Swedish, female cousin. Gingerly, Daniela reached down and grabbed the wig. She picked it up and held it for a few moments, staring at it dazedly. Then I heard her murmur something to the wig, just under her breath: "Have a safe trip back to Sweden, Cousin Olaf. Send a postcard." Then she leapt over to me. Plunking the wig squarely on my head, she cried, "Hit it!"

She took her position and belted out the final stanza. Her red hair was flying everywhere. Sarah, Janine and Lisa might have been disappointed—but the *boys* in the audience weren't!

> *Teachers tell us a cover shouldn't make us judge a book,*
> *And we should all just take another look.*
> *A new trick for studying or the latest tattoo trends;*
> *You never know what you can learn from new friends.*

Sometimes things aren't always what you see,
Surprises where you don't expect them to be.

Everyone joined in as Daniela sang the chorus one last time. Eldrick finished the song with a final flurry of thumps. He tossed his drumsticks in the air catching one behind his back and the other in his mouth. And we were done! Holding hands we took a bow and waved to the audience. I took the Olaf wig off and threw it into the audience. A tearful Lisa caught it. Grabbing hands again, the BEDMAS Conspiracy left the stage. We immediately surrounded Daniela.

"Are you okay?" the four of us asked in unison.

Daniela looked both elated and stunned. "Sarah, Lisa, and Janine are going to kill me. Not to mention the basketball team who had Olaf playing point guard next week."

"They'll get over it," I said. "What about you?"

But the shock had apparently worn off by this point, leaving her just plain old happy. She grinned at me and flashed me two thumbs up.

Next, I turned to our drummer and caught him up in a bear hug.

"Eldrick! Why didn't you tell me you could drum like that?"

"There are a lot of things you don't know about me," he said smiling. "Hey, Sludge!"

Sludge had joined in the hug.

"You're back!" I said, giving him a high-five.

"Yup. It was so weird, man! One minute, I'm up on stage staring at a watch, and the next minute, I'm in the crowd watching you guys onstage. And Gary's beside me and he's freaking out, yelling 'Chicken Licken! Chicken Licken!' at the top of his lungs. Looks like someone's beaten him up pretty good, too. He has a big black eye."

He turned to Daniela. "Nice to have you back, Red," he said to her with a wink. "Always thought you looked better as a carrot-top."

"Never knew you'd make such an awesome chicken," said Daniela, grinning. "*Cluuuck, cluck, cluck*!"

And as the whole band stood together, it was hard to tell who laughed the loudest.

$$(^2 / x + -)$$

It turned out that chicken jokes never got old.

Even weeks after the competition, no one could

look at Sludge without letting out a long *cluuuck.*

Eldrick had taken to calling Sludge his fowl-mouthed friend. Meena referred to him as her barnyard buddy.

We sat in my garage, jamming and joking.

"I'm getting hungry," said Daniela after a few songs. "Anyone up for...wings?"

We all cracked up.

"Yeah, that's one for Helen the Hysterical," grumbled Sludge.

Mercifully, I changed the subject. "So have you guys decided what you're going to do with your share of the winners' cheque?"

In the end, the competition had been close but, our final song, "Unexpected Surprises," had put us on top.

"It's one thing to write a great song, but it's something else to let the audience really *experience* it," one of the judges told us after the show. "And the BEDMAS Conspiracy's performance was definitely an *experience*!"

"I'm taking a summer course at the Fashion Design Institute," answered Meena. "I am so sick of mauve. I've been saying for months that green is the new purple."

We waited for the echo from Beena.

"Space camp!" she declared unexpectedly. "There's a big universe out there and I want to explore it a bit."

"And what about you, little guy?" asked Sludge, throwing his arm around Eldrick. "I saw the way Lisa Hutchin looked at you after the show. You gonna use some of your cash to take her out?"

Eldrick blushed a deep crimson. He smiled shyly and the light glinted off his new braces.

"I'm sure she won't mind the metallic teeth," said Sludge.

"Actually," said Eldrick. "I got a phone call last night. It was the guys from Metal Mouth. You're looking at the new drummer for their summer Bar Mitzvah tour."

"Nice!" we all agreed.

"So," I said, changing the subject. "Looks like I might need some help if I'm going to ace Friday's science test. After all, I've got a B average that I'd like to hold on to."

Eldrick's eyes instantly lit up. "Science? No problem!"

"I've read the chapter but I'm having trouble with the terms. It would be awesome if we could come up with a song to help me remember some of the words."

The Z's nodded and grabbed their instruments.

"What's the topic, buddy?" asked Sludge.

"Whatever it is, I'm sure it won't be hard to come up with a rhyme," said Eldrick confidently.

"Great!" I answered with a grin. "So...anybody know what rhymes with *electromagnetism*?"

More adventures from J. R. Wilcott Middle School

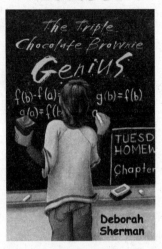

Michael is lazy, unmotivated, and the most popular president ever elected at J.R. Wilcott Middle School. But one day, he eats a whole pan of his mother's triple chocolate brownies. Before he knows it, Michael has become his worst nightmare—a know-it-all and a brainiac.

Something doesn't add up!

Don't miss this prequel to
The BEDMAS Conspiracy
by Deborah Sherman.

Backstage with Deborah Sherman
★★★★★★★★★★★★★★★★★★★★★★★★★★★★★★★

What is your musical background?

I have never been in a band but I did play the piano when I was a kid...that is, of course, until my piano teacher suggested that I "take a break" from playing. I'm not really sure if I had any piano talent because I never *ever* practised.

If I could play an instrument in a band, it would be the bass. Then I could hang out at the back of the stage, play a few notes, and have fun.

My favourite band is probably Death Cab for Cutie. My little girl is a Feist fan because she counts to four in one of her songs!

If you had to pick one character from *The BEDMAS Conspiracy* that you were most like in school, who would that be? Who inspired some of your characters?

The inspiration for Adam was probably my husband. I saw one of his old report cards where his teacher called him a dreamer. He was (and is!) a smart guy but he never really focused on what the teacher was saying or on studying for tests. Whenever we walk by his grade school, I always point to the window and joke that's the window he stared out of all day long.

I was probably a combination of Eldrick, Sludge, and Adam: Eldrick because I actually didn't mind studying; Adam because math was my worst subject; and Sludge because I had a bit of a devious streak...although nothing to land me in the back row of detention for a month.

Which character was the most fun for you to create?

Sludge is always fun to write. He is a goof but a goof with a big heart and (perhaps to some people) surprisingly intelligent. I love a character who is full of surprises. Sludge is full of surprises. But so is Eldrick. He is much more than people give him credit for at the beginning. I work as a teacher, so every year I meet a handful of kids who are a bit different. Sometimes those kids aren't always as appreciated as they should be....at first!

You've done quite a bit of travelling. What are some of your favourite places to visit?

Italy is one of my favourite places to visit because it is so historical and the food is delicious—the best pizza ever! And, nothing can top walking on the Great Wall of China during Chinese New Year. But one of my favourite vacations took place camping in the Maritimes.

If you were going to compete in a talent competition, what would your chosen talent be?

That is a tough one. My students would tell you that drawing is NOT one of my talents. (In fact, just yesterday, one of my students demanded that I take drawing lessons from him. He is five! Though he did teach me how to draw a pretty good cruise ship.) Tap dancing sounds fun, though.